THE
SMALLEST
CREATURES

A fateful road trip full of murder, mystery and
suspense

DAN MCNAY

THE
BOOK
FOLKS

Paperback published by The Book Folks

London, 2017

ISBN 978-1-9735-9087-3

www.thebookfolks.com

The smallest creatures,
As every night they do,
Come to the edge of them...

James Dickey

For my kids: Heather, Chris, Allie, and Chelsea

Prologue

The rain fell in endless heavy waves in the dead-end alley. The only light was from a hooded bulb over the back door of the club. It was midnight. George paused to look up before stepping outside onto the concrete platform. He would always be handsome, looking younger than thirty-two, his forehead wrinkled in amusement. Stepping out, he held his hand above his eyes to look for something or someone. His leather jacket was instantly soaked. He turned up his collar and came down, holding onto the old pipe railing. There was a flash of a red sequined dress behind him in the doorway. Someone brought him an umbrella.

"George!"

He turned on the soaked pavement, his wide shoulders dark from the downpour. A car roared. Tires slid. No headlights. It hit him directly in the back, shoving him into the platform and the railing. He didn't make a sound. The car backed away immediately, all the way back to the street, and was gone. He was on the ground. There was something dark oozing from underneath him. There was a scream.

Chapter One

The black figure paused against the bright doorway, waiting for the screen to slam behind him. He eased through the cluttered well of the courtyard to a gray icebox next to the gray fence, and tugged at its handle. No light inside. Removing a can of beer, he returned to a chair that sat like a shadow before the screen. He popped it and gurgled the beer. When he bent to set the can on the cement, his chest seemed wide and empty, almost cavernous, as if he were all silhouette and had no depth. Striking a match dispelled the illusion. The flame, drawn to a cigarette, exposed his forehead and long nose. Beads of perspiration glistened on his yellow skin.

The match was waved out. Again, the hot night enveloped him like a mother swaddling a child for sleep. He shifted on the chair, pulling from his pocket a folded piece of paper. The orange ember of his cigarette bobbed as he opened the letter. His head bowed, but unable to read the gray sheet, he held it up so that the paper grew translucent, glowing against the doorway. The writing there was large, sprawling and awkward. It was addressed to him.

dear david,

How are you I am fine Mama tolb me to write you ond tell you you wont see no more. Mama anb daddy gut me on a list for a home I go soon Mana tolb me il will be nice aut I bont know I miss you and stuff

ooo Xxx
Carolime

Pe Come get me plaese.

As he folded the letter and stuffed it back into his pocket, the ember of the cigarette trembled in his fingers. He sighed, exhaling smoke. The white and then gray cloud curled over his bent shoulders. Flicking away the cigarette suddenly, he stood, leaving the beer to turn back to the bright room.

Inside, the thick odor of turpentine overwhelmed him once more. He steadied himself against the headboard of the bed until the nausea passed. Squeezing down between the bed and chifforobe, he took up the brush in his meaty hand and began trimming the wall above the freshly painted baseboard. His head was already throbbing. Paint dribbled back over his fingers, splattering the floor and wet molding. He jerked the brush away, but paint flew everywhere. The sickly bitter taste was on his tongue and lips.

He spat. Reaching for the rag behind him, he furiously wiped at his hands and the brush. Splotches were on his arms, his clothes, and the floor – paint on everything. It wouldn't come off. He stiffened in revulsion. "God damn it!" He stabbed the brush at the baseboard. "I can't! I can't!"

He stabbed again and again, and then threw the brush at the screen in rage.

His anger quickly crumbled. The mess he had made was beyond redemption. The sheets on the bed were smeared as well. And there was no one here to cry to. No one to tell him to calm down, count to ten, and to look for a starting place to fix it. He was alone in a dirty room. He hugged his long legs up to his chest and hid his breaking face. "Fuck them all!" Remaining there, he rocked himself like a child after a scolding, lost in a blind blubbering pout.

In a little while, his rocking ceased, and he lifted his face to the stillness of the room. The window and door were open, but there was no air to breathe, no air to stir the sheet hanging from the bed beside him. The evening outside was languid. It hadn't rained in weeks. The sounds he could usually hear, the music from Bourbon Street and the traffic buzzing in the opposite direction, were gone. The river and the breezes that loved it were silenced, dreaming beneath the humid blanket of night. Only his tears flowed. Once his face was drying, he could see with the calm clarity of exhaustion, and wondered why he had cared enough. No one cared about him. He was twenty-two and on his own.

There was a sudden rapping on the screen. David started. He was frightened and a bit embarrassed, but got to his feet quickly. He couldn't see who was outside, nor was he expecting anyone.

"Who's there?"

"Hello."

"Who is it?"

"Davey, it's me, Martha Greenly."

She opened the screen and helped her granddaughter climb the single step into the room. The little girl wasn't sure she liked any of this. Her nose scrunched up at the smell, changing her worried look to a grimace. Hiding her face in her grandmother's faded skirt, she must have been warding off the odor. Her suspicious gaze belied any shyness. The three-year-old's expressions, the brow drawn tight and the almost make-believe frown, were so similar to her grandmother's that David took to looking at her as a reflection, a confirmation of Mrs. Greenly's moods.

4

This time, however, the older woman was smiling. She seemed relieved to find him here. Her smile and bright eyes were incongruent with the face which was normally quite grim and unattractive. She never wore makeup or let her hair down. Tonight was different, the smile had changed her; she looked human. Her skin was still taut although given to wrinkles around her mouth and eyes because of her constant agitation. She might even be called pretty. He guessed she was around forty. David was nervous. In her drab way, she was flirting with him. She had to be after something.

"We had a devil of a time finding you. You've been crying!" She reached up to lay her palm against his cheek. "And you're hotter than blazes. Are you all right?"

"It's nothing." He was blushing.

"Are you sure? If there's something you want to tell me, you can, you know. We're friends."

"No really. I'm fine."

"I didn't mean to embarrass you. I'm just a nosey old woman. It's none of my business. Boy, is it smelly in here. You should have a fan to blow the fumes out. No wonder you're not feeling well."

"What are you two doing out so late?" he asked.

Her smile loosened and nearly fell.

"Don't you remember your offer? I wouldn't have gone to all this trouble to track you down, if I had known you weren't serious. Those directions you gave me were wrong. I had to knock on three doors before I found somebody that knew you. It's not safe out there at night for a woman and a small child to be roaming around. I might have gotten hurt – then what would have become of Lisa?"

"I remember my offer."

"You're acting mighty odd about it."

"I'm in the middle of painting."

"How about this weekend?" she asked. "You said any time, but if you're busy, Lisa and I will have to wait, I guess. This looks like a big project. You could probably use some help yourself. I wish I could give you a hand – that way you wouldn't feel so put out about helping me – but if we're going to have to wait, I've got to find another place to live. Mrs. Pierce told me I can't be the building manager after Sunday. We just can't sit on our furniture out on the sidewalk until you can see your way clear to move us."

"Do I have a choice about putting it off?"

"I tried to get hold of you earlier, I really did. But you've got no telephone over here. The print shop where you work told me they didn't allow any personal calls. What was I supposed to do?"

"It's all right. You found me. When will you be ready to go? Friday night?"

I'm sorry to have to put you through this. It's not fair to take your whole weekend after you've worked hard all week. If there were any other way... but you're all we've got!"

"Tomorrow night?"

"I'm worried about that car. I don't know if it will hold up for the distance. We would be in an awful state if we got stranded someplace along the way. Do you think you could look at it and tell if it needed work?"

"I could try to get off early tomorrow."

"We'll need to load the trailer tomorrow night. I was thinking you could come right now."

"I'm in the middle of painting."

"Please, Davey."

"Oh, all right. Let me get my shoes on."

David opened the flimsy door of the chifforobe and pulled on a t-shirt to cover himself. Carrying his shoes and socks to the bed, he sat on the only clean corner, and began putting them on. He was hoping she would step outside to wait, so that he could have a minute to breathe and to rub his tired face awake, but he knew she wasn't going to budge. When he bent to tie a shoelace Mrs.

6

Greenly gave him a peck on the forehead. He looked up at her startled.

"That's for being such a good guy."

"I haven't got you there yet." Blood was rising to his face again.

"You will. I have no doubts about it. Oh. I checked the bus schedule and there's a bus that leaves Nashville at ten o'clock Sunday night. It arrives here at five the next morning."

"What makes you think I want to sleep on the bus?"

"I wish there were some other way."

"We can leave tomorrow night."

"Well, we can certainly try. Won't you be tired after working all day?"

David shrugged.

"We'll try, I promise. We'll be exhausted from packing and loading and Lisa will be out of sorts, but if that's what we have to do —" She placed her hand on her granddaughter's head. "Then we'll do it, won't we, Lisa?"

The little girl glanced, from him, up to her grandmother, without understanding what had been asked. When she shook her head, Mrs. Greenly giggled. "She's tired."

Lisa buried her face back into the folds of the skirt, hiding her eyes as well this time.

David got to his feet impatiently. Why were they asking this child for an opinion? He was tired himself. Mrs. Greenly had never treated her like a person before, so why get cutesy now?

"Well?"

"Oh." Mrs. Greenly grabbed the little girl's hand and turned quickly to the screen. David followed. His headache, which he had hoped belonged to the fumes he had been breathing, accompanied him outside. He held his head with one hand as he half-heartedly swung the outer door closed.

"You forgot to lock it," Mrs. Greenly said nervously.

"The furniture," he muttered.

"Someone is sure to go in and take your clothes."

He looked at her.

"Is something wrong?" she asked.

Not up to arguing with her, David turned back and shut the door, closing the padlock on the latch.

"I don't mean to be telling you what to do," Mrs. Greenly said, as she waited for him at the screen that led to the front hall. He held the door for them without comment. The coolness of the foyer seemed to ease his throbbing scalp, despite the stench of urine and tobacco. The hallway light was out again and when they entered the clammy darkness Lisa tripped over a piece of plaster from the wall. Mrs. Greenly's grasp checked her stumbling.

"This place is terrible. I don't see why you wanted to move over here," she said.

"The room in your building smelled of cigars. I couldn't get rid of it."

David opened the front door for them. Following along the narrow sidewalk, he quickly became impatient as they slowed to avoid the front stoops and signposts. He stepped out to walk beside them in the gutter. The charcoal pavement was a trough of seclusion, contained by walls of worn plaster and the darker textures of brick and wrought iron. This was where life had run out, leaving the street bone dry in the night. Other than the streetlamp at the corner, the only light to shape them was the yellow glow seeping from between the slats of shuttered windows. When they stopped at the corner, David's shadow engulfed the woman and child. They looked both ways for Lisa's sake and then crossed. The light of the streetlamp, which had never left the slope of his shoulders, slipped like mercury down over Mrs. Greenly, and fell on the little girl's tightly parted hair. Her pigtails were snowy white, the floss of a little grandmother waiting on a church step. He glanced from her to the woman's determined face bobbing in the shadow of his arm. Her anticipation made her different, out of place here. Hadn't she been like him – a stranger in a photo taken for local color – someone to be pitied in passing? David couldn't imagine Nashville or the trailer she had there, but he would take her just the same. It was important to have something, even if it was only a place and not a person.

"You heard anything from your daughter?" he asked.

"I can't think about it. She never gave one thought to me or her own little girl. It's all right that I've worried over this one. She went off with her friends and drank away our money. And she tells me: but we'll always have a roof over our heads and food to eat. Miss Smarty-Pants. Now I'm losing everything. But it's all right, she says. That's her answer to everything. And she's probably lying stone cold in the back of some godforsaken alley."

"Don't worry, I'll get you to Nashville," David said. "Maybe she's in jail or broke and stranded somewhere."

"Don't you start."

"What?"

"Don't you try to tell me it's going to be all right. It'll be all right when it's over and I'm tucked in a grave."

"You shouldn't say that."

"Why? Am I scaring you? Oh. I'm not being very nice, am I? Just ignore me, I'm a worrywart at heart, nothing makes me happy."

"How will she find you if she turns up after you're gone? Is there someone over there to leave a letter with?"

"She knows where the trailer is, if she isn't already there. More than likely, she's lying on a sunny beach in Florida. She's always talking about Florida." Mrs. Greenly frowned. "She was always talking about Florida. You're going to get hit by a car if you keep on walking in the street."

"There isn't any traffic."

"Look. I got enough to worry about. You got to take care of yourself, for our sakes if nothing else. Or think of the example you're setting for Lisa then. What happens if she decides she wants to do what you're doing? What happens if she gets hit? You don't ever think!"

He paused to let them walk on ahead, and stepped back to the curb. Mrs. Greenly glanced over her shoulder with approval, but her smile was quickly hidden by the glare of approaching headlights. A car had turned on to the street at the next intersection. There was something wrong with the way it was driven. Its mass, concealed by unwieldy and blinding beams, rushed at them, swerving along the pavement. He reached for her arm in apprehension. At his touch, she turned to his exposed face and suddenly moaned, throwing up her hands to shield herself, as if his face was the source of the insensible light. The car roared by them. He looked at her again, his eyes hazed with the blue smear of afterglow. She was trembling, but she lowered her hands. What had he done to her?

"Are you all right?" he asked.

"Let me catch my breath."

"Stupid drunk. He's going to kill someone."

"Please. Let's just go look at the car."

"I didn't mean to scare you."

"I'm real jumpy is all."

"What –" he started to ask, but she dismissed him with a curt wave of her hand and hurried on, pulling Lisa after her. He followed, perplexed. Her anger was very unfair; he hadn't meant to frighten her. All he had tried to do was protect her. If she was already thinking the worst of him, then maybe that's how he should treat her. She seemed to expect it. Surely she wasn't as crazy as she was acting.

"How much further?"

"It's right here," she said.

She was pointing, with a slight smile, to the break in the concrete wall ahead. They entered the forlorn lot, her heels clacking before him with the hollow sound which verged on an echo. The car was across the open pavement, sitting alone in a back corner. It was a ten-year-old Ford

Galaxy. The chrome and dark blue paint were stained and the tires were low. Above the dent marring the front fender, a smear of mud fanned out over the hood and windshield. The car was a weary sight for David. He was reminded of those derelicts his father would drag back into the gravel patch behind the house. Some were rebuilt. Some were cannibalized: their chassis left to be consumed by the summer weeds. This car had been deserted too long. He couldn't imagine it starting or even being driven a short distance. How could she be pleased with such a miserable prospect?

She was digging in her purse for the keys. They were handed to him with that same attitude of anticipation, except now, the hard crest of her determination was replaced by something softer, something open and a bit precious. He nervously opened the door and maneuvered his long legs under the steering wheel. The interior reeked of old whisky. He held his breath and rolled down the window on the passenger's side, but it didn't help. There wasn't a breeze. Pretending not to be nauseous, he turned the key and listened to the engine churn without starting. He tried a second time, again without success. A drop of sweat trickled from his eyebrow as he played with the choke and gas pedal. The engine convulsed over and over and over and over and became whiny. The interior light, left on by his open door, dimmed. He stopped and then reached for a cigarette, only to find he had left them outside his room.

"You think it will start?" Mrs. Greenly asked.

"Sometimes it helps to count."

David tapped his fingers on the steering wheel and tried to imagine how long it took to smoke a cigarette. Finally, but too soon – a cigarette lasted longer than this – he pushed in the choke, pumped the gas seriously, and turned the key once more. The engine dragged and caught, starting sluggishly. He nursed the gas to bring the drunken gasping up to a roar. And then exercised the roar until it seemed strong. Slowly letting up on the pedal, he listened

11

and hoped for the engine to settle into an idle. When it relaxed willingly and continued to run, he was elated. Patience had to be a virtue.

He looked up and found Mrs. Greenly's face broken open in a smile. She was almost ready to jump up and down and clap her hands. He smiled too.

"How long has the car been sitting here?"

"About two months. Ah, I think. I mean I'm not sure when my daughter drove it last." She turned to her granddaughter. "You ready to go traveling, Lisa?"

The little girl yawned.

David climbed out awkwardly and joined them in watching as the car shivered and chugged.

"You think it will make the trip?" Mrs. Greenly asked.

Without answering, David began to circle the back end, as if he were examining the car carefully. He was looking. The rear was rusted badly and the tires were worn. He held a hand to the exhaust and found only a slight film of oil on his palm. On the opposite side, the paint was wavy from body work. When he came around to the front, Mrs. Greenly helped him open the hood. He peered into the engine's greasy crevices. It seemed to be running smoothly enough. The battery was corroded and the fan belt was old and loose, but other than that, he hadn't the vaguest idea of what he was looking at.

"It'll do," he said finally, unable to prevent himself from lying. The dishonesty embarrassed him. He wasn't like this. What was he trying to gain? Her fears about being stranded weren't groundless. The car probably would break down. She would really be overjoyed with him then. David knew he should tell the truth and he would be off the hook, but he couldn't. Her belief was all he had. He hoped that somehow his pronouncement about the car would make it come true.

"I'm glad to hear that," Mrs. Greenly was saying. "I was afraid it would need all kinds of work. So we're ready to go, you think? Except for loading the trailer."

"Yes!" he said. "Ah... why don't we take a little spin?"

"I need to get Lisa home. She's tired."

"I'll drive you over."

"What would you do with the car?"

"What do you mean?" he asked.

"You'd bring it straight back here?"

"Sure. I don't have anywhere else to park it."

"And you'll walk the keys back over to me?"

"I thought you said you didn't know how to drive."

"I haven't done much."

"That's a long walk and I need to clean up from painting. What do you need the keys for? There won't be anything you can do until I get off work tomorrow."

"I trust you, Davey. But something could happen to you. There's a lot of crazy people out there. It might not even be your fault. What if nothing happened to the car, but you were hurt at work. How would I get the keys back? Am I supposed to run around the city with Lisa in tow, trying to find —"

"All right!" David interrupted. "It's your car."

Crawling back into the front seat, he stretched across to roll up the passenger's window, and then turned the ignition off. The engine knocked a bit and died. His angry effort to make sure the door was secure went unacknowledged. He wanted to be fair, but her guarded acceptance of the keys confirmed his suspicions. She thought he wanted to steal the goddamn thing.

"You've got to understand. I do trust you. This business with the keys isn't a reflection on you. I wouldn't get in the car with you at all, let alone let you drive us to Nashville if I didn't trust you with my life. You're a good boy. And you're smart enough to realize you've got a foolish and frightened woman on your hands. I wouldn't want to put up with me."

"I'm not sure I want to."

"I'm sorry. It's just that if something happened to the car now, I think I'd go out of my mind." She was smiling.

"You wouldn't want to cause me to have a nervous breakdown, would you?"

"I suppose not."

Her smile was seductive. "I knew you'd understand. You're not like the other men I've known. I know you're tired, but would you mind walking us back to our building? It's sort of scary out here at night."

"All right," he said, trying to keep his voice even.

When Mrs. Greenly reached for Lisa's hand, the little girl raised both arms for her grandmother to pick her up.

"You're too big for Grandma to carry. You'll have to walk." She looked at David. "She's tired. It'll take forever to coax her to walk all the way back. Do you think you're strong enough to carry her? You'll get rid of us quicker."

"Sounds good to me."

He lifted Lisa up. She laid her head on his shoulder immediately, as if she had known him all her life. With her thumb in her mouth and the other tiny hand on his chest, she closed her eyes and was apparently going to sleep. She wasn't as heavy as he thought she would be. As they left the parking lot, the fine hair of her pigtail began tickling his nose. He shifted her gently so that he wouldn't sneeze. Even though she was a warm and pretty urchin, he was embarrassed by the physical contact and the predicament of carrying her past the bars where he usually drank. All he needed was for some of those people to see him. His only option was to tough it out. He couldn't make her walk now – she trusted him.

"I knew you would be good with her," Mrs. Greenly said.

"You're not like the rest of the bums here. You're going to make a good papa one of these days."

"I'm never getting married."

"Oh, what do you know?"

"Kids are a lot of work. You have to teach them everything."

"And they still don't learn," she said, half to herself.

"Love is for dummies."

"Love is something you can't help. It's worse if you've been hurt. Was that why you were crying before we got there tonight?"

"I really don't want to talk about it."

"You're sensitive. You seem like you'd have a lot to give to the right person."

"I ain't got nothing to give," he said.

His venomous tone silenced her. He had done what she wanted, now she could leave him alone for a while. He was too tired to talk. And his arms and back were beginning to ache with the weight of the girl. As they crossed another intersection, he tried to remember how much farther they had to go, but he couldn't count the blocks or recall how many there were. He'd be damned if he would ask Mrs. Greenly. Why wasn't there someone else to tell him the distance, the number of black streets to cross, how many doorways to ignore, and how long he would have to walk? He had been left here, hadn't he?

Chapter Two

David angrily finished the plates on the two color press and threw his sponge at the bucket. Water splashed out onto the floor. The puddle was going to be a hazard in reaching the rear of the press, but he refused to clean it up. The son-of-a-bitch couldn't slip and fall down anyway. The press ran again, and when the man came back, he deftly sidestepped the problem, just as David thought he would. The make-ready runs continued, the hopping up on the press, the cleanings, the adjustments, and then the hopping down to either end and the momentary rush of rollers. And then the hopping up again. They worked without speaking, both ignoring and avoiding the puddle as if it was a necessary part of getting the job done. Finally, worn down by the endless repetition of his chores, David grabbed some rags to sop up the spill.

"You want to clean up —" his boss started to say, looking up from the latest printed sheet.

"What?"

"I'm going to get this approved. Be right back."

His absence meant a break for David. It seemed long overdue. The make-ready run had gone on forever. He tossed the rags into the puddle and lazily stirred them with his foot until most of the water was absorbed. Once David's boss was safely out of the room, Mel stepped off his press and sauntered over. David looked away and wished he would disappear.

"How old is this woman you're going to move?"

"It matters?"

"Maybe she's around forty? Red hair and gorgeous eyes?"

"You have to make everything a dirty joke?"

"I'm just trying to figure you out."

David thought of the way Mrs. Greenly looked, but couldn't really guess her age. She was somewhere in her forties or fifties.

"She's old enough to be my mother!"

"You go for an older woman, you don't fool around."

"Go away."

"I can hear her: Oh David, you're such a sweet thing. And so young!"

David shoved him.

"Get away from me!"

"You don't push me, you hear! Just 'cause you're bigger, that don't make you tougher."

"Shut up if you don't want trouble."

"Who the hell do you think you are to be shoving people around?"

"All right!" David's boss shouted at them.

"I was only joking, for Christ's sake," Mel told the pressman. "He gave me a push. I almost fell down."

"Get back to your own machine and stay put. And you!" he said to David. "Get those plates ready!"

David held his tongue and did as he was told, but it wasn't easy. Who did his boss think he was yelling at? He had some goddamn nerve, walking into the middle of it. He didn't know what was going on. David was cleaning the top, angrily punching the on button to jog the rollers forward. The corner of his sponge caught between the two large drums. Cursing, he yanked it free, and finished. He had started on the bottom, when the pressman came up for something on the shelf behind him.

"It's not my fault!" David said.

His boss ignored him and walked back along the platform to the front of the press. David jabbed away at the on button. The son-of-a-bitch! Not paying attention, he held the button down too long. His hand slipped – his middle finger was in the rollers. He screamed and jerked it free. The throbbing rushed up his arm. He leaned back and cupped the hand in his lap. Tears filled his eyes.

Everyone came running. His boss was standing over him.

"Let's see."

David held out his hand for their examination. The pressman gingerly turned the palm up.

"The finger," David told him.

"Yeah. That's all. You were lucky."

David withdrew his hand to his lap and tried to move the finger. There was a sharp pain that lingered.

"Don't move it," his boss said. "You'll have to go to the doctor. Come on out to the edge of the platform. I'll go find out who you're supposed to see."

David left the press. Once his coworkers were assured that it was a minor injury, they dispersed, going back to their own jobs. Only Mel remained. He picked up the sponge David had dropped and gummed the offset plates.

"The way you yelled, I was sure you had run your whole arm up in the rollers."

"Really?"

"I bet they could hear you in the warehouse. You should have been here when Doyle had his accident. The press was running full speed. He broke four fingers and the skin popped open on the back of his hand right here. Blood was all over the place. He was out almost three weeks." Mel dropped the sponge into the water bucket. "They put me with your pressman. Maybe I'll get to be over here the rest of the day."

The pressman returned with a card for David.

"I gummed the plates for you," Mel said.

"This is the address," his boss said, ignoring the other helper. "It's down Carondelete, a half block before Canal. You think you can get there by yourself?"

"Sure."

"Well, don't worry about coming back today."

"There's someone you can pull from the bindery?"

"Yeah," his boss said.

David awkwardly stuffed his cigarettes into his pocket with his left hand and went out.

Squinting into the bright hot sun was disconcerting after the darkness of the loading dock. His escape seemed odd, out of place, as if it were a memory or a dream barely recalled. He glanced back at the dock, but couldn't penetrate the slab of shadow. Was someone watching? He turned away, suddenly spooked, like a child frightened by the night. They didn't like him. He wouldn't be missed. He wanted to run, but was afraid the movement would make his finger throb even more. Why should he go to the doctor? The sun was shining in Jackson Square. There would be pretty girls taking pictures. He paused at the corner where the streetcar would stop, but then decided not to wait. He had to go, his hand was becoming a mess. At least the finger could be fixed.

David hurried now, protecting the hand by holding it at his shoulder. They had to be able to heal it. The injury wasn't completely his fault. He knew he shouldn't have let those guys get to him. He shouldn't have lost control, but what was he supposed to do? No one was going to ride him! This time would be different. He wasn't going to punish himself. The doctor would do something – make it heal right, so there wouldn't be a reminder. He wasn't doing the whole goddamn thing over again!

The blue and white sign pointing the way to the hospital's emergency entrance reassured him. Everything would be fine in a little while. He entered the heavy sea of sunlight cast from the windows. Beyond the swirling dust was a girl at a desk, bent over some paperwork. Her shoulder-length hair falling across one cheek seemed to his darkened eyes a crisp shade of rust against the snowy blue collar of her uniform. She didn't notice him. Her preoccupation made him timid.

"Ah, excuse me," he said.

She looked up and smiled. She was pretty. Did she have freckles?

"I'm David Jacks. I think my boss called to let you know I was coming."

"No one called me. What's the problem?"

"I had an accident on the job."

She got up abruptly and retrieved a wheelchair from the corridor.

"It's only my hand," he said.

"Relax and enjoy."

Despite his embarrassment, David allowed her to wheel him across the lobby. When she turned to back him against the wall, the quick swing of the chair made his finger throb again. He murmured an 'ouch' and grimaced. She apologized and then asked for the name of his company, telling him she would have to call to verify his insurance. After placing the call, she returned with a clipboard.

"Everything is fine. The doctor will see you as soon as these forms are completed."

"I can't write. I hurt my finger."

"Oh."

She sat down and went through the questionnaire with him, checking off his replies as he gave them. He was flattered by the attention, but her beauty frightened him. It was as if he was expected to live up to the way she looked, and was failing. Her hair, blonde in the sunlight, didn't have a trace of red. He had been mistaken. Unable to meet her glance, her eyes blank with grace, he watched her tuck a strand of hair behind an ear. Her fingers were small, childlike and smooth-skinned. His were grotesque in comparison. He hadn't been able to wash before leaving work. The fingers and nails were blackened and stained with ink, and rough from repeated scrubbings. And now the one finger was swollen all out of proportion. He wanted to hide them. Suddenly realizing that she was looking at them too, he became flustered. She was waiting for a reply to a question which he hadn't heard. He blurted out a no, hoping that the answer was somehow appropriate and wouldn't make her laugh. She checked it off routinely. Completing the history, she held the clipboard so that he could sign a release, and then left him. Only a whiff of something sweet remained.

He wasn't used to girls who wore perfume. A lot of them did, he realized, but he hadn't seemed to notice until now. She had gone back to her paperwork. A raised eyebrow and a finger absently twirling a strand of hair reminded him of those smart girls in high school. She was competent and a hard worker – the kind of girl he ought to marry. Housework and children wouldn't be difficult for her. She glanced up and caught him watching her. Flashing a curt smile, she turned away. Her typewriter chattered at him efficiently. David chastised himself for staring. He was being stupid. She was probably a nurse, or studying to be one. Why did he think she might be interested in him?

He wouldn't look at her anymore. Outside, beyond the plate glass window, the traffic ran by silently, as if he were in a vacuum. The gleaming sunlight reminded him of other smells: those flowers they would break off and suck for the nectar when they were kids; or the raspy odor of straw. It was her perspiration – it was her freckles. Her arm in the light from the loft door. He rubbed his eyes and glanced at the girl at the desk, but couldn't see her now. The edge of the shadow had retreated, leaving him uncovered in the sun.

A chair scraped and the girl entered the bright well, crossing to a television beneath the window. Her hair seemed white now, the color of cobwebs. After selecting the proper channel and turning up the sound, she returned to the darkness without even glancing in his direction. He could hear the television; two doctors were discussing a serious case, but he couldn't see the picture. All that the glare permitted was the reflection of himself in the wheelchair. Moving closer was impossible; his finger was throbbing again. He couldn't wheel the chair over with one hand. How long was he expected to wait? He didn't want to sit here all morning with nothing to do. He didn't want to think about anything. This whole thing was stupid. He wasn't a goddamn invalid.

"Excuse me! Miss!" he called.

"Yes?"

"How about getting this show on the road!"

"The nurse will be out in just a minute."

When the woman appeared, David quickly got out of the chair. He wasn't going to be wheeled about any more. He was already enough of a fool. She escorted him back, assisted another nurse in taking an x-ray of his hand, and then left him in a large examination room. Again, he was made to wait, this time with his finger pulsating from the extra movement. He looked around at the beds and equipment impatiently. Was he expected to sit here with nothing to do? There wasn't another client in the whole place. What were they doing? Just as he stepped out into the corridor to find him, the doctor appeared.

"I'm Doctor Halle. I won't shake hands," he smiled. "Come over to the table."

David allowed his hand to be cleaned.

"You've got a hairline fracture at the end of your finger. Not so serious. You'll have to wear a brace until it heals."

"I can still work?"

"Sure. But you should try to keep it clean."

A long aluminum brace was slipped down over the finger and secured with tape. Before releasing his hand, the

22

doctor gingerly turned it over, exposing a large scar which ran diagonally across the palm.

"I cut myself with an axe."

"Can you touch your little finger with your thumb?"

David demonstrated that he could.

"It doesn't hurt?"

"It's just a bit stiff."

The doctor shook his head.

"You ignore a wound like this and you come to me for a tiny fracture?"

"I was being stupid."

"You could have gotten a major infection. You're a lucky fellow."

Chapter Three

David was wheezing and gulping for air when he rang the buzzer. He had run most of the way. The long evening shadows and the fumes and noise of the rush hour traffic were swallowing the street. The taste of soot was on his tongue. Inside, beyond the door, he imagined her anger swelling in the rank rooms. She'd think he wasn't coming. He inhaled slowly and deeply to prepare himself and rang again. Someone was opening the door. She peered up at him from the crack. Then she scowled. Her hair was covered by an old dishrag, and cotton was stuffed in both ears and up her nose. He couldn't help but grin.

"You look like the dragon lady."

"I've been cleaning. Dust makes me sneeze," Mrs. Greenly said. "Where have you been?"

"I fell asleep. I had an accident —"

"I knew it. I thought I was having a premonition last night when I said something might happen to you. What did you do?"

David held up his finger.

"You're not going to be able to use your hand, are you?"

"Don't you worry about me," he said, suddenly angry. "I can do anything I have to."

"I've been worrying about you all afternoon. You should have called to say you were going to be late. How would I know if you were really coming or not? You could have been just having a good joke at my expense."

"Oh yeah, I get my kicks taking advantage of old women."

"I'm not that old, am I?" Her face grew suddenly sad. "I'm sorry, Davey. You're right. We shouldn't be fighting. Does your finger hurt?"

"A little."

"Everything is too crazy. Trying to get the car ready. Mrs. Pierce, who owns the building, has been bugging me. And I think Lisa's coming down with something."

"I was going to come over earlier, but I fell asleep."

"I can't take all of this. I really can't! Next time you'll call, won't you?"

"I was asleep..."

Mrs. Greenly was looking distractedly over her shoulder as she held the door for him. He stepped inside the large dingy hallway.

"Anyway," he said, not sure if she was listening. "I've gotten some rest, so I'll be able to drive tonight after we've finished loading."

"We'll talk about it later. I've got company," she said. She looked up at him. "Don't you think it's high time you called me by my first name."

"I guess. It's Martha?"

She nodded and then motioned for him to follow her into the apartment.

Inside was a short skinny bespectacled man. His thin wrists, hanging from the baggy sleeves of his suit jacket, made him seem frail. He smiled tentatively when Mrs. Greenly introduced them.

"Mr. Moore is with the Police Department," she added. "Mrs. Pierce called him to tell him we were moving."

"I'm sure she meant well," the skinny man said. "You hadn't called."

"I've been busy. She gave me absolutely no notice. Trying to find another place and taking care of Lisa hasn't been a piece of cake. I would have let you know as soon as I was settled."

"Still no word from your daughter?"

"Not a peep. Not that I want to hear from her, mind you. But I'm having my new number listed, and I've let everyone know where the new place is, so if she wants to find me, she can."

"Where exactly is this place you're moving?"

"Ah, over in the Irish Channel. About three blocks toward the river from St. Charles on Louisiana. I can't rightly recall the street address. I've got it written down around here someplace." She looked pleadingly at David. "Do you remember the number?"

"Well, um...843 or 846, something like that." David felt his face getting hot under the skinny man's scrutiny. A blush would give him away, but he didn't know how to stop it.

"I'll call you Monday to give you the address," Mrs. Greenly said. "You haven't found the car yet?"

"It's still under investigation."

"It's probably parked on the beach in Florida."

"You'll call?" he asked.

"Promise."

"Well, I'll get out of your way. It looks like you've got a lot of work to do yet, if you're going to be out of here this weekend."

Mrs. Greenly followed him to the door.

"Nice to meet you," he said to David. "I'm sorry it has to be under these circumstances."

He left.

"What the –" David started to ask.

Mrs. Greenly had put a finger to her lips. Looking outside to make sure he had left the hallway, she then closed the door carefully and set the deadbolt.

"I don't like lying to the police," David said.

"Lower your voice." She looked toward the kitchen. "I'm sorry I didn't tell you what's going on. I didn't think there was any cause to worry you. Let me see what Lisa is up to."

She returned from the kitchen after a moment.

"I don't want her to hear," she whispered. "She's too young to understand and I don't want her upset."

"What is it?"

"A couple of weeks before you showed up here looking for a room, Lisa's father was killed. By a hit and run driver." Mrs. Greenly glanced at the kitchen door again. "The police haven't found the car. They think my daughter was involved."

"She killed her husband?"

"They weren't married. I'm not saying what she did or didn't do, you understand, but there was a lot going on then. They haven't found the car because I've got it! Don't you see – if I turned it in to them, they would impound it as evidence and then I'd never get free of this place!"

"And what happens if we get caught? They'll think we did it! They won't let you keep the little girl in the cell with you."

"You can't make me stay here! I won't!" Her fists were clenched. "I'll drive the damn car myself. I don't need you!"

"Just calm down for a minute. Let me think."

"We don't have time to think."

"There isn't any other place where you could stay for a couple of days?" he asked.

"That won't help – even if I did know of somebody."

"We could buy some stolen plates or maybe have the car painted. Or at least load up and leave from a place where we won't be seen."

"It's been almost two months, Davey. They're not watching me."

"How would you know if they were or not."

"I'm not stupid."

"You're not very honest either," he said.

"There's the door if you want to go."

"Why do you make it so goddamn hard for someone to help you?"

"We're two peas in a pod, Davey."

"Well, I'm going to go out and look around for your friend. If I so much as even smell a cop, I'm gone. You can find some other patsy."

"Why don't you bring the car while you're at it?" She retrieved her purse from the end table and found the key. "It's across the street behind the filling station. The attendant was kind enough to go get it and hitch up the trailer I rented from him this afternoon. He's a real good guy."

"If he's such a sweet guy, why don't you have him drive you?"

"Are you jealous?"

"Of what?"

She wasn't going to say what. Perhaps she didn't have to. The laugh lines about her eyes were crinkled in amusement. Her look was warm and real, more genuine than any he had seen in months. The slight advantage she seemed to have didn't even bother him. She had a potential attractiveness that was hard to dismiss. Her eyes were deep and dangerous. It was just the rest of it, her old shapeless clothes, her bare face and the cotton in her nose and ears, that made her a witch. He shook his head as if to tell her: oh no you don't.

"You are the dragon lady."

His hand was on the doorknob, ready to make his escape.

"Don't call me that anymore," she said. "I don't like it."

Had she said anything else he could have gone freely.

"I'll get the car. Be back in a minute."

He pulled on the knob, but nothing happened. It wouldn't budge.

"The bolt," she said.

"Oh, yeah!" He laughed in embarrassment, fumbled with the latch and let himself out.

Hoping to appear nonchalant, David lit a cigarette on the front step and blew smoke rings into the descending air. Dust was settling on the sidewalk. The flood of traffic was gone, leaving the uneven flow of stragglers, commuters late for dinner. This wasn't the time to be waiting. He walked toward the far corner of the block, retracing the way he had come earlier, and examined the empty interiors of the parked cars. Just as she had said, there was nothing to be found. At the corner, a ragged man sat in an old Cadillac, a piece of rubber tied around his bicep, a plastic syringe in his hand. David turned away before the man could notice him. Suddenly he realized that all this time he had been carrying the keys in his hand, tossing them absentmindedly as he walked. He looked around frantically and started to stuff them in his pocket, but then stopped. There wasn't any point. If someone was watching, they had already seen him with them. His fingerprints were all over that car! How could he be so stupid?

He didn't know how to be a criminal. All he had thought to do was use up an otherwise drunken weekend. Now he was out here pacing the sidewalk like some maniac. You had to be able to lie and not give a shit, like she just did with that cop. And she wanted David to call her by her first name. As if he didn't know whose benefit it was for. She had to be crazy to think he was buying everything she told him. Even if it did sound reasonable. They probably weren't watching her. They probably had a thousand other cases to worry about. This was only one open file, but it was the one with you in it. The file with the handcuffs, the wire grid between the front and back seats, and the heavy door that closed you in with the homosexuals.

He wanted to tell himself it was all nonsense, but he continued to look. His ears might be burning, the back of his head alive with goose bumps, as if something or someone was watching, but he wasn't going to give in. He wasn't going to go crazy! The curtain of that window hadn't moved. The people driving by weren't slowing to look at him. The junkie hadn't even raised his head. David couldn't understand what was happening to him. He had never been so scared. If protecting yourself – wanting to know if they were coming for you – wasn't insanity, then why did it feel that way?

A decision would have to be made: he was nearing the station at the corner. He paused, not bothering to take one last look around; in a moment it wouldn't matter if they were there or not. The attendant glanced up at him from the windshield he was cleaning. David avoided his look. He would have to be a fool to go ahead with this. He should give the keys back, go to his room and finish painting. And drown in the smell of turpentine. There really wasn't much of a choice, was there. He went to get the car.

It started easily enough this time. And as he pulled out into the street, the empty trailer bouncing over the curb, there weren't any sirens or plainclothesmen on the run with their pistols pulled. He felt as silly as a child who had fallen out of bed. A couple of turns around the block brought him to a parking space which would accommodate the car and trailer and wasn't far from her door. He locked the car carefully and bounded up her front steps. She was waiting for him in the living room.

"I asked a couple of the tenants to move their cars so you could park. Did you get the space?"

"Yep. I thought it was a happy accident. Thanks."

He glanced around the room for things to start loading. Nothing seemed touched.

"The boxes in the kitchen?" he asked.

"How am I supposed to get boxes with Lisa on my hands?"

"Well, I can buy some from the station. They usually have them."

"I can't afford to go buying any boxes."

"You want me to just load the stuff in there loose?"

"Not on your life! I don't want everything broken."

"Why don't you have anything ready?"

"There's a couple pieces of furniture in the bedroom _"

"This is just plain stupid."

She paused indignantly.

"I've been cleaning."

"I don't believe this! How am I supposed to move you? You're not thinking!"

"You're the one with the crazy notion of leaving tonight and driving all that way without any sleep. I'd say that was pretty stupid. For your information Mr. MacIntyre and Toni are coming down to help us get your precious trailer loaded. If you're through throwing your weight around, maybe you'd like to go find us boxes to pack with."

The little girl came out of the kitchen just then. She was filthy. Her hair, coated with dust, was the color of murky dishwater. There were stains on her dress and her face was smeared. David felt sorry for her. The woman neglected her as badly as she neglected everything else. And he would have said as much, if Lisa hadn't been in the room.

"Nana, I got to go potty."

"Ok, dear."

31

Martha scowled at him as she took the little girl's hand.

"Shit!" he muttered, and throwing up his arms, stormed out to look for the boxes.

David had to buy the boxes from a liquor store down the street. It wasn't a lot of money, but it was his money. He got the boxes down to the sidewalk without dropping them, in spite of the flaps cutting into his bare arms. The faded "Rooms For Rent" sign was swinging viciously above the stoop.

That it didn't fall seemed miraculous. The thing was attached to the eyebolts in the canopy by two thin strands of rusted wire. The sign should have fallen long before he had first seen it. Perhaps he'd knock it down before he left. Pulling the boxes up to the door, he let himself in and took them to her apartment. Old Mr. MacIntyre, who had lived here forever, was on the couch tamping his pipe. His knees stood high above the coffee table: two knotty joints of bone barely hidden beneath the shiny cloth of his trousers. He nodded soberly and puffed, enveloping his wobbly head in smoke. Martha came out of the kitchen.

"You ever rent my room?" David asked her.

"Toni took it. She liked it better than her own after you did all that cleaning."

"His nose must not work well."

"Yours must work when it wants to," Martha said. "Where did you get these?"

"At a store down the street."

"Those Orientals aren't the cleanest folks. I quit trading there because of the cockroaches." She was pulling the boxes apart and shook one upside down to see if anything would fall out.

She handed him a list and money.

"We need a few things," Martha told him. "Would you mind taking Lisa along? She's been cooped up all day." He pocketed the scrap of paper and the bills. Lisa looked up at him.

"Don't buy the groceries at the same place you got these, ok? There's a store two blocks back on Governor Nichols that's much cleaner. A white couple own it. You would just have to wait to start loading the trailer anyway."

"They've got white cockroaches?"

"Well, do what you want. You will anyway."

David took the little girl's hand. Guiding her outside and down the steps wasn't hard, but once they were on the sidewalk he saw that they couldn't continue to walk hand in hand. He would have to lean sideways all the way to the store.

"Can you walk by yourself? I'm too tall and you're too short."

She nodded gravely. He released her hand and regretted it immediately. Her feelings were hurt. Digging in his pocket for the list her grandmother had given him – he had thought to give it to her to carry – he found he had pulled out Caroline's letter. Fatigue and sorrow filled him. He ought to throw the damn thing away, but it seemed stuck to his fingers. Stuffing the letter away, he located the list and the money and stopped.

"Here. I want you to hold on to these for me. Put them in your pocket so you don't lose them."

He helped her hide the money and they went on.

Turning off the wide dry street, they walked back into the narrow avenues of the quarter. Doors were open here, and he glimpsed the empty living rooms and the further doorways of all the bright kitchens. There were sounds of dinner: inarticulate chatter, pans and dishes clattering and the chirp of laughter above the humming floor fans. A television talked. Before them were two fat black women sitting on their stoop. Their foreheads glistened with the sweat of stoves and the frying popping dinner newly done. One lazily adjusted the bra strap beneath her housedress.

"Well, hello cutie," she said to Lisa. Both women smiled up at David when the girl grasped his pant leg. It was hard to smile back, to share in their appreciation of her shyness – there was something wrong in a fearful child – and only after he had passed their door and its strong whiff of baking cornbread, did he manage a nod, one which was only safe to give because he knew they couldn't see.

The smell of cornbread had reminded him that he hadn't had dinner. To be hungry and to be home again, to smell dinner from the back screen as you washed up, and to enter the hot kitchen with your face and hands still wet. To do nothing but sit down and eat, while your mother moved from stove to table. She will be in the kitchen always, her bangs plastered to her forehead, the cotton dress clinging to her limbs, serving meals of plenty without tenderness. This was her privilege. How she would ridicule the concoctions the men would make when they raided the refrigerator after church. With him, however, there had been a promise of favor. And he would wait forever for the tokens, the hurried smile in passing, her hand patting the table beside him, or the bemused look. It was only now that he knew that the promise had been a lie. She couldn't accept their willingness. Even as a child he hadn't been allowed to help. For Caroline it was the same wherever she went. When they were small and she was there for dinner they would sit at the corner of the table and build houses out of playing cards as his mother cooked. Caroline would laugh with joy as he knocked them down.

And he would walk her to school in the morning and bring her back each evening. Over the same route every day. Four blocks to the top of the ridge where the railroad ran and then to the right, down the road beside the grade. He wasn't allowed to take her the easy way, on the footpath around the little house back through the weeds and down the granite cut to cross the tracks. They would walk the road, shuffling their feet in the gravel dust of early autumn or in the brown leaves as winter approached, and wave to the trains on their way to the underpass where the concrete walls were streaked with wax like drippings of soft black tar. She had put him up to chewing it like bubblegum once. In the autumn her hand would be sweaty, in winter soft and warm. After school, the other boys would tease them and run. He envied their freedom, but rather than complain, he would take her behind the bakery across the street, and standing beneath the window fan, they would share the sweet smell of bread and she would pretend he was her boyfriend.

He had been, hadn't he? Even then in innocence. So what if she was slow? Her world didn't look like everyone else's. He had quickly passed her in school – she was two years older than him – but her problems had never bothered him. It was her pain! Long ago, at a party in the thick grass of someone's yard, a brightly colored piñata had been hung for the children to take turns at whacking with a baseball bat. None of them, except for David and her, were large enough or strong enough to break it and as she refused her turn, the papier-mâché horse danced and twisted forever. When he finally made his swing – going last – the candy came spilling out and the children ducked and scrambled for their shares. David jumped in as well and, because he was fast and fearless, emerged with a full bag. He found her standing, still holding herself back, with tears running down her cheeks, as if her whole life had fallen from the belly of the paper horse. Sharing his bag with her had dried her eyes, but it didn't seem to make up for anything.

"Does your Grandmother let you have sweets?" he asked Lisa.

She nodded.

"What kind do you like?"

"I don't know."

"When we get to the store we'll have to look. You remind me so I don't forget."

As they neared the corner, the bright melody of the steamboat calliope wafted across to them from the river, the momentarily clear snatches of music mixing and dancing about the sounds of the traffic and the apartments they passed. For it to be playing this time of day was odd. The cathedral in Jackson Square was joining in, chiming the beginning of a new hour. While the time was measured off by the repeated tone of a solitary bell, the rim of the great whirlpool of birds rose and fell in the deep sky behind the rooftops. They circled the square with every toll of the bells. The music spoke of home, not of a home that he knew or would ever know, but of something lost before memory began. He almost wanted to cry. And he wished he could be in the square right now, to watch the mass of grey and brown wings rising above the evening sun like a phantasmal carousel climbing and escaping the grass and stone and the spires of the iron fences.

Lisa's hand had grasped the seam of his pant leg again. Suddenly realizing that they had stopped in the middle of the sidewalk, he glanced at her to see if she was worried by his behavior. She had been watching the birds, too.

"They're pretty," he said.

She nodded.

"Are they a parade?" she asked.

"Well, something like that."

They found the store and went in. Martha Greenly had been right, it was cleaner than the other one. He retrieved the list from Lisa's pocket and they gathered the groceries. Even though he had the girl help him carry a couple of items, he soon had his hands full and his finger was throbbing again. He hurried them to the counter.

"You forgot to remind me," he told her when he noticed her expectant gaze.

He took her back to the candy rack to pick out something. The man at the register didn't seem the least bit disturbed by their delay. After bagging the groceries, he bent over the counter to carefully place the change into the girl's small hand.

"I've got two of my own," the man replied to David's look.

Outside, dusk was closing in rapidly. He held her hand as they walked back even though it was awkward. She wouldn't have to be afraid of the dark as long as he was here. They were friends now. She gobbled the candy bar, licked her fingers and then wanted to be picked up.

"You sure you can't walk?"

"Carry."

He lifted her and settled her on his hip, grabbing the bag from the sidewalk with his other hand. She held the metal brace on his finger as if it were a saddle horn. His arms, already tired, were strained in trying to maintain her and the groceries. He didn't think he could get very far this way.

"You know how old you are?" he asked.

She held up three fingers.

"You can count? How far can you count to?"

She counted to ten in one long quick breath.

"You're real smart."

"Remember when you yelled at the car?"

"No. Are you thinking about last night?"

"When it was raining."

"It wasn't raining last night. You think I'm somebody else?"

She didn't know how to answer that question.

"You're thinking I'm your daddy?"

"I don't know."

Her little frown appeared as she tried to figure out what she was remembering.

"I'm David, honey. I used to live upstairs."

His arms were aching now, but he felt he couldn't put her down without betraying her. Pausing to reestablish his grasp, he plodded on to the front steps of the building.

Mr. MacIntyre let them in. David put her down in the living room, next to some boxes which looked like they had been packed. Lisa scampered ahead of them into the kitchen. When David followed the old man back, he found that they were indeed packing. Martha was on a footstool, handing glasses down to Toni. This was the boy that David had thought was a girl. Even unshaven, he looked feminine. Toni glanced up from the box he was filling, and self-consciously put a hand to the scarf that covered the curlers in his hair. Was he blushing?

"This is great!" David told them. "You'd think somebody was moving."

"We had candy, Grandma," Lisa piped in.

"It looks like it." Martha stepped down to wipe the girl's face with a wet rag from the sink.

"I'm going to start loading those boxes into the trailer," David said.

"There's a bureau in the bedroom that should go in first. Toni can help you with it," Martha said.

Toni just stood there, smiling sheepishly.

"Well, come on," David said.

The bureau was in the back corner, sitting in front of a doorway. Its top was covered with an array of makeup and medicine and dirty underwear. As they cleared the things off, their reflection in the high mirror made Toni giggle. David looked to find himself elongated and slightly askew, a funhouse apparition in the company of a clown. The glass had settled oddly. He sent Toni to find a screwdriver while he pulled the piece out away from the wall. The wood joints creaked quietly when it was jostled. He was trying the door behind the bureau when Toni returned.

"I think that opens into another apartment," the boy said, handing him the screwdriver. "Can you do it with your finger in that thing?"

"You want to?"

Toni held up his hands timidly. His nails were long, sculptured and painted red.

"Never mind."

He tried the first screw and it came out effortlessly. The others were routine.

"You work in a show on Bourbon Street?" he asked him.

"I sing a little, and dance."

"Dressed up like a girl?"

"It's a female impersonator club. I'd look pretty silly dressed in boy's clothes."

"You like boys?"

"What else is there?" Toni smiled. "Do you have a girlfriend?"

"That's none of your business."

"I was only trying to make conversation. You've probably got a dozen."

"Sure," David said.

"I'm going to be a girl one day. I've already started taking hormones and having electrolysis."

"Really?"

"There's an operation you can get that will change you all the way."

"Sounds like loads of fun. You want to give me a hand?"

They lifted the mirror free and leaned it against the wall. Getting it out to the trailer wasn't going to be easy. Toni was straining just to hold the bureau off the floor.

"Put it down for a second," David told him.

They removed the drawers and laid them across the bed.

Atop the clothes in the last one Toni found a picture frame with a cracked glass. He held it up gingerly.

"Look. Here's your brother."

"Don't be silly," David said.

"Look."

David took the picture. The man in the photograph did resemble his older brother, but he was too thin and too sly. He was posed with a pretty blonde whose round face

David didn't know at all. They were dressed up, as if they were going to the senior prom. This wasn't his brother.

"You know who these people are?"

"George and Kathy."

"George and Kathy who?"

"I thought you were George's brother," Toni said.

"No," David examined the photo once more before putting it back into the drawer. "They're Lisa's parents."

"Yeah."

"He looks like a smart-ass," David said.

"He wasn't."

"Come on."

They maneuvered the bureau out of the bedroom. Mr. MacIntyre held open the outside door and they carried it up the sidewalk. When they emerged from the trailer both Toni and David were wet with sweat.

They paused to cool off.

"Can I bum a cigarette?" Toni asked.

"Sure."

"Are you from here?"

"Southern Indiana. Near the Ohio river," David said.

"Mrs. Greenly said you're driving her to Nashville. You'll be almost home."

"I suppose."

"Are you going to go visit while you're there?"

"I've got to be back to work on Monday," David said.

"I'd go visit if I had the chance." Toni cracked a sad little smile. "I guess I'm homesick."

"Really? Well, I guess everyone feels that way. Everyone that leaves home anyway."

"Or gets kicked out," Toni said.

"Or gets kicked out," David repeated.

"They all think I'm sick. They won't even answer my letters."

"Where's this?"

"St. Augustine."

"You just have to forget it and get on with your life."

"It's hard when you're alone as much as I am. I thought I would make friends with the other girls at the club, but they're all such bitches."

"It must be rough to meet normal people doing what you're doing."

"You've got sensitive eyes, did anyone ever tell you that?" Toni said.

"No. Nobody ever did. We'd better get back to work."

David put out his cigarette and started back. Toni caught up with him on the front steps.

"I hope I wasn't bugging you," he said.

"I need to get this trailer loaded," David told him.

David turned on the juice. He would lift as much as he could possibly carry, two or three boxes at a time, and rush them down the hall, down the front steps in a bound and up to the trailer to slide them in. He ran back. Toni tried to match his pace, but soon tired and perched on the hood of the car as David made a couple more trips. Toni followed him inside reluctantly.

"Sorry I'm not more help."

"Nobody can keep up with me once I get going."

He was wet and winded and happy. Sure he was showing off. His slender helper wasn't competition, in fact, Toni practically was a girl. And why shouldn't he show off? He had the muscles.

Flexing his arms and stretching, he bent for the last large box. By the time Toni offered to help he had already picked it up.

"Well, you certainly are the man around here, aren't you?" Toni said.

David nodded.

"You want some ice tea?" Toni asked.

"Sure."

Toni sidestepped Lisa, who was pulling a box by its flap through the kitchen doorway. As David balanced his load on the arm of the couch to get a better grip, he noticed the little girl's struggle with the box which was too heavy for her.

"Why don't you get this one here," he told her, pointing to a smaller one.

She could pick up the second box. He coaxed her to go with him and took the time to make sure she got down the front steps safely. The darkness outside didn't seem to bother her now. She marched steadily up the sidewalk in front of him and deposited her box at the curb beside the trailer. Standing as stiffly as a doll while he loaded the boxes, she turned and walked back beside him with a similar air: a child's idea of being a soldier. She gave no sign of wanting to hold hands or be carried. It was almost as if she were under orders. Had Martha put her up to this? He offered a hand when they reached the steps again but was politely refused with a shake of her head. She climbed ahead of him, filled with some grave responsibility. David hoped she wouldn't notice his amusement.

Mr. MacIntyre was setting another box on the living room floor when they entered. He looked up and tried to grin at Lisa, but his painful struggle to stand upright made his toothy smile malicious. She ran off to the bedroom. With a hand on the small of his back, he joined David, who was standing near a glass of iced tea on the coffee table.

"That's yours," Mr. MacIntyre said. "She's such a sweet little girl, considering."

His face seemed a bit too close to David's shoulder. He was sucking on his false teeth, the drawn mottled skin of his cheeks twitched slowly, thoughtfully. David drank part of his tea before replying.

"How's that?"

"The goings on here."

"You don't say."

"You don't have to believe me if you want."

"What goings on?"

"The little girl's parents. There were people in and out of here all night long. Not the sort you'd want to have around a child. And the fights. They'd be screaming and yelling and breaking things. They didn't care who heard."

"That so."

"They say the mother was a hooker."

"You wouldn't know about that first hand," David said.

"You think you're real smart, don't you."

"No sir. This whole thing is getting too crazy for me."

"Well, I was just telling the story. I didn't mean to put the fear of God in you. You're doing a good deed."

David nodded, sat down his glass decisively, and went after the box the man had brought out. He felt as if he had been violated. Mr. MacIntyre had stood too closely, exhaled his stale breath in his face and told him things he didn't want to hear. The old fart should have minded his own business. David knew he shouldn't have stopped to listen. His fatigue was slipping in now – the box he was carrying up the sidewalk seemed the heaviest one so far. What he had been told did make sense though. It explained a lot: the little girl's shyness, the cop's interest after all this time, and even the broken glass of that photograph and the nicks in the bureau. As David neared the car, his eyes fell on the front fender, the dent there, and the smear fanning back over the hood. He stopped. Jesus Christ, he thought. He could almost feel the thump of the body as it crumpled across the metal and glass. What the hell was he doing here? He shivered violently and hurried on to the trailer.

When he stepped off the curb, he saw a man running towards him from across the street. It was the station attendant. He was shouting something as he dodged through the traffic, but David couldn't hear him. David tossed the box into the trailer. The man reached him, panting for breath.

43

"A guy took something out of your trailer! He got into that old Cadillac at the corner."

"Where?" David demanded.

They stepped out into the street and the man pointed out the car.

"I called the police."

David ran for the Cadillac. It was at the far end of the block and he became winded while he was still some distance away, but he strode on, walking quickly now instead of running. He paused in front of the car long enough to hold his arms out from his sides, the palms open, to show that he wasn't armed, and then approached the driver's window. Inside was the wiry man in a large dirty overcoat. This was the junkie he had noticed earlier. The man's face, dark and greasy and with a tuft of hair below his lip, was still turned ahead toward the windshield when David tapped at the glass and at his own shallow reflection standing above the car. The man looked over. There was no reaction at all in his face. The window came down.

"You've got something of mine," David told him.

"Not me, man."

"We saw you take it. I want it back. Now!"

"You're mistaken."

"The cops have been called. You give it back and you can drive away. Otherwise we'll wait for them to get here."

"I can drive away?"

"Just give me the goddamn thing."

The man opened the door, got out and reached behind the front seat. Drawing out a small box, he handed it over.

"You promised no cops, right?"

"Get in the fucking car and drive," David wanted to swing at him. "You should go to jail for stealing from an old woman!"

"Didn't realize, man. Sorry."

44

The little man climbed into the Cadillac, started the engine and pulled out cautiously. The car quickly disappeared into the snarl of taillights. Barely aware of the recovered box in his hands, David started toward the trailer where Martha and Mr. MacIntyre were waiting. The realization of what he had done was only now sinking in. He could have gotten himself killed! The guy was a junkie. What if he had a gun? What if he decided to come back? This was stupid, stupid, stupid. He didn't want to die. Why had he taken the chance? He wasn't a hero. He was just lucky enough to get away with it.

Mr. MacIntyre clapped him on the back when he reached them.

"That was a very brave thing to do, my boy. No telling what might have happened."

"It wasn't real smart," David said.

"You should have let him keep it," Martha told him as she took the box. She sat it on the floor of the trailer to open the flaps. "All that's here is an old iron and one of Lisa's dolls. Hardly enough to go risking your life over."

"How was I supposed to know what was in it."

"It doesn't matter —"

"The man from the station was amazed at you," Mr. MacIntyre interrupted. "He said he had called the police."

"You should have waited for them," Martha said.

"Are there more boxes ready?" David asked.

"In the bedroom. You go ahead. Someone should thank the attendant. I'll be right back." She crossed the street.

Fuck you too, he thought, watching her go.

"You mind keeping an eye on things out here? Just so it won't happen again." David asked the old man.

"Could you bring my pipe back when you come? I left it laying on the coffee table. What you did was a brave thing, you know."

David nodded and headed back to the building.

He found Lisa, in her pajamas, waiting all alone in the open doorway of the apartment. She was scowling and near to tears, but when she saw him her face brightened.

"Hello," he said.

She hugged his leg. David patted her head absently. He didn't want this responsibility.

"Your Grandma went across the street for a minute. She'll be right back."

Where was she? He needed to finish loading the trailer. What was he supposed to do with the little girl? He couldn't leave her here. There were footsteps on the stairs behind him. David turned. Toni, in drag, smiled and waved and threw his arms wide.

"What do you think?" he hollered from the last step.

He was dressed up like a gypsy: curly long hair, hoops in his ears and a frilly peasant blouse with a sash and skirt. He was carrying a guitar case. David thought he made a very pretty girl, but he was too distracted to say so now.

"Hey. You think you could stay with Lisa a minute? I've got to move the car."

Toni was not pleased.

"I can't," he said. His heels echoed in the high hallway. "I've got to go to work."

David picked Lisa up and followed him to the front door.

"You do look nice. It would only be a second," David said.

Toni's face softened.

"I really can't. I'll be late. Are you leaving tonight?"

"Tomorrow morning probably."

"If you get done early, why don't you come catch the second show? I'll buy you a drink."

"If I live that long."

"It's next to Fritzel's. You know where that is?"

"Yeah."

They had come out to the front step. Toni said something else as he left, but David didn't hear it. In the street next to the car and trailer was a police car, its red lights revolving, flashing, blinking at him, over and over again. The old man was with one of them at the curb. There was no place to hide. David held his breath.

Chapter Four

It was like waking from a bad dream. After Mr. MacIntyre had pointed him out, one of the cops called to him. He picked Lisa up and went down, not expecting to return. Throughout their questions his guilt oozed from every pore and he was sure they noticed. He was ready to blurt his confession – ask forgiveness for the car, the fight with his father and the piece of pie he had once snitched from a restaurant – but they didn't seem to suspect a thing. They returned to their patrol car and drove off. He wasn't arrested! He would have laughed in his giddiness if the old man hadn't been there.

MacIntyre had eyed him curiously anyway. The scent of good gossip must have been too apparent to ignore. He offered a remark about how the police made everyone nervous, but David simply smiled and bit his lip. Being so close to admitting all, David was tempted to let him in on the truth, but he could see what the result would be. The old man's face was already anticipating who he might tell about what had happened. David refused to contribute to some whispered and leering story.

But he could tell someone, couldn't he? Once Martha returned to put Lisa to bed, he found himself rushing again, impatient to be finished with the trailer and ready to be free of their company. The restlessness, like the aching of a shipwrecked man, nagged at him, and by the time he had moved the car and returned the keys to Martha's safekeeping, he was repulsed by the thought of his room. He needed to talk – it didn't matter to whom. A confession wasn't really necessary. Everyone was talking about the weather right now anyway. He started for Bourbon Street, to look for someone he knew.

The faces there were always the same and always different. The tourists who thronged the narrow pavement, their eyes and smiles alive with the arcade lights, were indistinguishable from those who walked in their steps the previous night, yet they resembled others he had seen before. One looked like the owner of the hardware store where he and his father used to trade. Another could have been a cousin at a church barbecue, another a neighbor's sister. The people who worked the street, the hot dog vendors, the barkers and the bartenders were more concrete: they had personalities and names. But they too were transitory. A face, which grew familiar in one setting, might suddenly vanish and then reappear in a week or two behind a counter down the street. Some slipped away for good, their absence only noticed much later in the fleeting thoughts of an uneasy night.

The barker out in front of Toni's club was one of the faces that he knew but hadn't missed until now – upon finding him here. They had drunk and played pool at a bar on Dauphine and then David didn't find him there anymore. The fat boy grinned as he brushed the limp hair from his forehead. "So, you think it's going to rain? You want to take in the show?"

"I was thinking about it. A guy I know works here. Toni."

"Toni? Sure. Let me take you in and get you a fix with the waitress. You know Toni, huh? She can be real foxy when she wants to be."

"She's a guy."

"Whatever turns you on."

"Guys don't turn me on."

"Well, it's a good show anyway."

The curtain was drawn aside for him. He stopped in the doorway, lost in the well of darkness and the walls that danced with fire.

"Will you look at the long drink of water that moseyed in, girls," a falsetto voice boomed at him. "And just how big are those shoes you got on?"

He located the real speaker from the mirrored reflections that surrounded him. It was a huge and old drag queen in an orange dress. She had petticoats and ribbons and bows. Her face was wrinkled and painted in glaring colors to match her outfit. When she moved in the red spotlight she was Little-Bo-Peep packed in tomato paste.

"Well, come on in. We won't bite...too hard."

David wanted to run away, but he felt the fat boy's hand on his back, so he moved forward to find a table.

"We've got such a show, ladies and gents, so relax and enjoy. It's all for fun. I'm your MC and will be back later... to accept money or gifts. Traveler's checks are welcome."

The music started and she danced and skipped around the stage, lip-synching the words to *I Enjoy Being a Girl*. His beer was delivered as the small audience was applauding hesitantly. In the brief silence which followed, he was told that the beer was on the house. The waitress even refused his tip. When he glanced back at the stage, he found the drag queen staring at him and then, in the highest voice she could manage, she recited a poem.

"Georgie Porgy, puddin' pie,
Kissed the girls and made them cry,
And when the boys came out to play,
Georgie Porgy ran away."

David dared not look over his shoulder. If no one was behind him, it meant she was talking to him. Why me, he thought, shrinking down in his chair. He was a bug stuck to a board by a pin. Everyone was surely looking. She blew him a kiss from those sickly orange lips and ran from the stage. The music began again.

When David turned to look for his waitress, he found Toni standing at the servers' station, talking to the barmaid. When he reached over the counter for something, his raised heel caught the light and glistened in the mirror beside him. The curve of his rump seemed almost painfully perfect. David glimpsed his face in the glass behind the bar as he stood up, but it was soon hidden again in the shelves and the rows of bottles. Watching Toni made him nervous. David felt as though he had stepped through to another place where the rules had all changed. Like that book about Alice he had read to Caroline years ago when they used to go to the treehouse. Later, when they were teenagers, he had found her one evening in front of her mother's bureau, her face inches from her own image, her hands flat against those other cool hands, as if she were trying to measure her vision against the seamless surface of her other self. In her eyes there were blind spots which weren't blind and he could never quite understand what she could and couldn't see. Or perhaps she was looking for a way into a world not confined by glass.

His waitress had returned to the bar and he gained her attention with a wave. Toni was still turned away, but now he had moved or a bottle had been taken down and his reflection was exposed. He was talking happily to someone. Behind him, another performer had come on stage. As the music and the turning shards of light flowed over the dark arc of the liquor cabinet and the changing rainbow bottles, the space there seemed a fantastic altar or a threshold to a place where all of them were held captive. How they yearned to be freed, to be loved.

And there were Toni's eyes looking out at him without recognition. The blank gaze chilled him. Was something between them that he couldn't see? Suddenly Toni's face brightened and he turned and waved to him. He was at his table in a moment.

"You just get here?"

"Yes." He had to shout over the music.

"I'm up next. You're going to stay and watch?"

"All right."

"If you want to stick around I'll buy you a drink when I'm through."

Pointing to his bare wrist, he looked at him questioningly. Toni shrugged.

"I've had my rabies shot," he said.

He felt foolish making such a stupid excuse. He was here, wasn't he? Going home to the smell of paint and those splattered sheets was hardly appealing, even if he did have to be up early. He nodded reluctantly.

Toni patted his arm and left, disappearing into the darkness at the end of the bar. The performer currently on stage finished and then came a moment of soft music as the lights came down to a pale blue spot. Toni strolled out with a stool and his guitar.

"Hello," he said, bending to the mike. After he sat down he tried holding a hand above his eyes to peer out at the audience but gave up quickly with a little smile.

"I'm the serious one. I get to make you sad, if I can. I wanted to be Bette Midler, but they told me my tits weren't big enough yet. If you all come back next fall maybe I'll get to tell dirty jokes. This song was written by a very good friend of mine. It's called Mary Magdalene." And he sang.

Because of the red flowers in the clay jar,
And the sunlight on the floor before my window,
I pause to take a breath from another lonely ache,
And watch my belly grow.
Deserted in the morning, alone in the chair,

We swell with the sighs that know
The creaking and the stretching of the wooden bed
Left empty in a room below.

How I was happy and willing just to cling,
You were so like a dogwood tree
White and soft in the spring.

His voice was gravelly, but it was sweet and sensuous
– and feminine. He seemed to be singing a lullaby to the
sulking chaos of the room. The ones who were talking
now stopped to listen. The sudden silence revealed the
squeak of strings as he changed chords, giving the melody
texture, like the chirps the newborn might reply to the
nesting bird's riff. The cigarette smoke hung low,
protecting him from perfect view and removing the words
to another place and another time.

As he bent to the microphone, his hair fell forward to
frame his face. He seemed on the verge of kissing the
metal. David was queasy and spellbound. The pretty face,
with its small nose and full lips, was wanton, but he knew
it for what it was: a mask. And now, the song, which had
reached so firmly into the secrets he held close, emerged as
a melody, a message, passing through him as if it were
being sung somewhere else by a shadow whose name he
knew.

The guitar trailed off into silence.

The audience stirred and then awakened. This was the
first real applause David had heard. Toni had become
more than a curiosity. He had entertained them. David
clapped as well, his big hands making a deep bass noise in
a cacophony of snare drums, but he was slowed by the
sadness he had swallowed. He stopped long before the
applause died. The song hadn't been easy to understand,
nor was he any judge of music. What he did hear was the
certainty of pain in the one left behind. The piped-in music
suddenly exploded around him. Toni must have gotten off.
And the MC was up there making an ass out of herself

again. David looked at the people around him, their sounds now buried in the blaring rock and roll. They were having fun. But at whose expense? He got up, hardened and angry with distaste, unwilling to be a part of them a second longer.

The door to the street was tempting, but he didn't leave. He had promised Toni he would stick around, and he would, despite the noise and the clutter. Retreating to the bar, he ordered another beer and watched the show through the mirror. It was better that way – the MC and the next performer were partially hidden from view – and he was separated from them. They became characters on a movie screen, something he could walk out on if he didn't like the story. After a little while, Toni appeared by his side and took his arm. He gulped down the last of his glass and accompanied him into the back bar. Were all the waitresses watching them?

More heads seemed to turn when they entered. The faces were stiff, as if the femininity they mimicked was the femininity of store mannequins. Some looked like lumberjacks made up for a burlesque. Others might pass as mothers and girlfriends in the hard light of day. But what he saw in their eyes belied all their studied appearances. There wasn't a trace of the swooning or giggling adolescents they might have been. They had never been cuddled children. They were here because there were no compromises. A tall stately blonde watched him brazenly as they took a table and continued to stare even after he frowned at her. Perhaps he was an interloper – there weren't any other men dressed as men in this part of the bar.

The waitress wasn't in a hurry to get to their table. Toni finally flagged her down so that they could order. Her apology for not seeing them seemed real enough. He had to be mistaken. No one had asked him to leave, had they? She delivered their beers and waved off Toni's attempt to pay her.

"Is she a guy too?" David asked.

"Not anymore."

"I just don't understand this. I'd better go."

"Relax, there's nothing to be afraid of. We're a bunch of sissies, is all. Nothing scary."

"Everyone is staring at us."

"Accepting men are hard to find here."

"What?"

"You're tall and rugged," he said. "They would all look feminine next to you."

"Jesus."

"So what did you think of the show?" he asked.

"It was all right – you've got a lot of talent."

He reached across the table to squeeze his hand.

"Thank you."

David pulled away.

"Sorry," he said, holding his hands up as if in apology. "What did you do to your hand?"

He looked at Toni quizzically. Hadn't he told him?

"I ran the finger into the rollers on a printing press."

"I meant the scar."

David was suddenly ashamed. He folded the hand down on the table, not knowing what else to do with it.

"I cut it."

"It must have been a pretty nasty cut."

"Yeah."

Toni waited.

"I cannot tell a lie. I did it wid my widdle hatchet." His wisecrack was too bitter to be funny. He hadn't laughed. "It's no big deal really. I just had an accident."

"Ok," he said, leaning forward to sip on the straw in his drink. He abruptly tossed his hair back from his eyes and looked at him. "You don't have to tell me about it if you don't want to."

"I..."

He softly touched the hand and withdrew quickly.

"It doesn't look as bad as you think," he said.

"I was holding the axe with my left hand."

"I'm clumsy myself."

"I can chop wood easier than most people can slice butter with a knife. They made fun of me once and I swore they'd never do it again."

"Who?"

"My father and brother. But they were doing it again. I got mad."

Toni seemed to want to smile at him and make some flippant remark to ease his anger, but he hesitated, holding his sympathetic grimace. David knew he was being an awkward hayseed – that whatever he had to tell him wouldn't compare to what Toni's own life had held. And he couldn't talk worth a damn. Toni had every right to think he was silly. What could he possibly say to express his feelings? If he could, he would have snatched his heart from the smoky air and rubbed it in Toni's made-up face.

Suddenly he was talking. It was as if he couldn't help himself. The words came tumbling and gushing like a creek pregnant with rain. He told Toni about the cold spring morning. How they had driven the pickup down to the last meadow, to the pile of lumber left stacked from the old barn they had dismantled that fall. How the weeds were stiff and crystalline in the sun and crunched beneath their heavy boots. His brother clapped his hands and held them before his white breath as their father tried to start the power saw. The cord was pulled and pulled again and finally the motor howled. Smoke whirled about his father's red jacket. He began cutting the first rafter into manageable chunks while David and his brother pulled them up to the ruts of the trail and chopped them down. It wasn't too long before his brother had laid aside his axe to load the wood into the truck. David usually ended up doing most of the chopping – and didn't care. He was the fastest. But this morning, left alone with his axe and all the wood, he became annoyed. He had a touch of something. His head was hot and his joints ached. Knowing that the fever would probably be broken by his sweat and exertion didn't make the chore any less grueling. And he couldn't say anything to them. When he had mentioned feeling ill at breakfast, his brother had accused him of trying to weasel out of coming. They wanted to make him feel guilty about not doing most of the work! Damn them, he thought. They would help soon enough once they realized he meant to take all morning.

His brother leaned against the truck.

"There's a new band playing at the Eagles Friday night," he told David. "I knew you'd just love to go, so I asked Amy to fix you up with someone. I told her you were real easy. Any girl that didn't drool."

"I don't think so."

"What are you going to do? Sit home and watch TV?"

"You should work that axe as hard as you do your mouth."

"Really. So what are you going to do Friday night?"

"I thought I'd take a walk over to see Caroline."

They both glanced at their father, who couldn't possibly hear their conversation because of the saw noise. He must have sensed their gaze. The sun glared from the lens of his glasses.

"What?" he shouted, looking from one to the other.

He shut the saw off.

"What?"

"I said I thought I'd take a walk over to Caroline's Friday night," David repeated.

"We've discussed this," his father said.

"I'm a grown man. I can make my own decisions."

"Your body's grown, but the rest of you hasn't caught up. You don't know the first thing about love."

"I know enough."

"Davey likes dummies," his brother said. "They don't give you any back talk." Then he added in a high voice, "Oh Davey, where do you want to put your hand tonight?"

His father was stifling a grin.

"Shut up!" David said.

"Davey. Won't you play that game where I take off my panties?"

"Damn you! Shut up!"

David brandished his axe.

"Enough!" his father said. "Get back to work."

"Neither of you know a fucking thing."

"Watch your tongue," his father said.

"Fuck you!"

His father put down the power saw and advanced on David.

"You don't talk that way to me."

"Sorry. Fuck you, sir."

His father slapped him. His face burned. Dropping the axe, David swung his open hand. His father's glasses were knocked askew and dangled from one ear. He was stupefied by what he had done. His father's fist flew into his face. The hard ground smacked against his back and head. He was down, his father standing over him in the frozen blue sky.

"You cool off!" his father said, straightening his glasses. He turned and walked away. David's left hand found the axe beside him. He grabbed it. His anger was as stiff and as cold as the ground. Not with this, something told him. Getting to his feet, he found a piece of siding nearby. He lifted one end and swung the axe. The blade was going to hit clumsily! He tried to yank the hand clear, but the axe bounced into his palm. Blood welled up around the steel and his body recoiled. The throbbing sent panic to his heart. Not now. Not yet. Forcing the hand back to the fiery wood, he swung the axe again and the stick came away free. He started for his father. His veins were pulsating, pumping his own blood out through the hole in his hand. His grip was hot and slippery. He raised the stick.

"Dad!" came the shout from behind him. His father looked up startled and then jumped back, out of David's shadow. The power saw was still buzzing in his hands. He tripped and went sprawling across the stack of beams. The saw fell to the ground, danced on its end like a child's top, and rolled on to his father's leg, ripping the overalls, ripping the flesh and ripping the blood out to mix in the dust. His father screamed. David couldn't move. Somehow his father had kicked the saw away. His brother was at his father's side, helping him and shouting at David. "Get the fuck out of here! Disappear!" David dropped the stick and ran toward the house.

"Last call," the waitress said over their heads. David and Toni looked up, disconcerted. They decided against one last drink, David was already feeling woozy. It was just as well that he was interrupted – he couldn't have gone on without telling how he left, how he didn't know if his father had lost the leg. He didn't want to know. He didn't want the judgment to fall.

"You ready?" he asked Toni.

"What happened?"

"I went to the house and grabbed some stuff and took off."

"What about your father?"

"I don't care," David said softly.

"Whew," Toni said, not sure how to reply. "I think I'm getting a little tipsy."

"You don't have much to say for yourself. What's with your family? They didn't like the boys you were seeing? You couldn't run for homecoming queen?"

"I don't think you're interested."

"You may be right. None of this stuff makes much sense."

"It's real simple. Just pretend I'm a girl."

"Like a fairy tale, huh? One swing with the old magic wand and everything is the way it should be."

"Something like that," Toni said.

"Well Tinkerbell, swing it in my direction, would you?"

"Why are you so mean?"

David frowned. The room suddenly became uneven when he stood up. He grabbed the back of his chair.

"Are you all right?" Toni asked him.

"Just point me in the right direction."

He took his arm and guided him through the show bar to the entrance. The fat boy was still outside, but as there were so few potential customers left on the street he had stopped grabbing them and was swinging his arms back and forth like a pitcher in a bullpen. When he gave them a thumbs up sign, David angrily jerked free of Toni's grasp and stepped into the street. A horn blared. He was pulled back by his shoulders just as a taxi rushed by in front of him.

"You trying to get yourself killed?" Toni demanded.

"Would it matter?"

Toni's fingers were still tightly holding his shoulders, his nails biting into his skin through his shirt fabric. This time, instead of twisting free, he gently lifted Toni's hands and turned around.

"I'm all right. Thank you," he said thickly. "They've taken the barricades down. It must be late."

"You're drunk."

"I was fine till I stood up."

"This way." He took his arm again.

"Good luck!" the fat boy yelled after them.

David waved his free arm in a backward farewell. As his feet seemed to be moving in the right direction he began to regain composure. He didn't need his help. What was he looking at, anyway? The street was nearly deserted, only the lonely neon lights and the falling silence lay ahead. The pavement looked glossy – almost wet.

"Did it rain?" he asked.

"I don't think so."

"Where are we going?"

"To the apartment house," he replied without a glance.

"Why?"

"Why?" Now Toni's eyes found his. They were dark with mascara and shadow, blue and bright in the artificial light. They were confident.

"I don't live there anymore," he whispered.

"Where do you live?"

"A couple blocks from here."

"You want to show me?" he asked.

"This way."

They turned the corner and walked away from the glare. Their shadows grew long and faded into the thick darkness. He stumbled.

"Damn," he muttered.

He stopped and lent his arm for support as Toni checked his heel. No damage had been done. After a tentative step forward, he continued their determined pace.

"You know, I couldn't ever tell if they loved me," he said.

"Who?"

"My folks. I wanted them to."

"We've got a lot in common." He paused beneath the streetlamp's soft glow and faced him. His hands were on his shoulders again.

"Everyone needs tenderness," he told him.

"I can't –"

"Just accept what's given you."

"Wait."

Toni started to look hurt, but then changed his mind and smiled.

"All right."

He took his arm and hugged it as they walked.

"Did you like my song?" he asked.

"It was sad."

"You don't think it was too serious? That was the first time I had ever sang it there."

"Everybody seemed to like it."

"George wrote it for me."

"Lisa's father?"

"Yeah."

"You must have known him pretty well," David said.

"We were lovers."

"But — you're a boy."

"You'll learn," he said quietly. "George did a lot of things because he had to — to survive. I was one of the things he did because he wanted to."

"You think I look like him?"

"A little. But he was as gentle as a moth. A girl at the club used to say that butter wouldn't melt in his mouth on a hot day. I swear she thought she was Scarlett O'Hara. He was very artistic. Those women just didn't understand that part of him."

"What women?"

"That bitch he pimped for and her mother. I think his girlfriend was the one that ran him over."

"I thought you and Martha were friends."

"I wanted to meet you."

Why had he said that? Did he really expect him to believe he had plotted to get close to him?

"I hope you're satisfied," he said.

"You're not ugly."

They had reached his building. He fumbled with his key and then held the door with his foot to say good night to her. Toni didn't appear to be leaving.

"You want to come in," he said, hoping to hear a refusal. He didn't answer. "Come in then."

He preceded him down the black hallway.

"I must be the most desirable man in the world."

"You're not George."

David held the screen door to the courtyard for him.

"We can sit outside," he said. "The room is a mess. I've been painting. You want a beer?"

"No."

He went to the icebox still sitting on the chair near the fence and got one for himself. It was warm, but he didn't care. He guzzled almost half before taking a breath.

"Let's go in," he said.

"It's a mess."

"I don't care."

He dubiously opened the door and pulled the cord on the bare bulb overhead. The room was just as he had left it. Paintbrushes were soaking in an open can of turpentine. The bedsheets were crumpled and splattered. A trail of tiny ants wound across the wooden floor from the windowsill to an empty beer can he had left at the foot of the bed. Despite the lessened smell, his head began to throb as it had the previous evening.

"I think I'm going to be hungover tomorrow," he said.

Toni waited as he slid the top sheet aside to make a clean place for him to sit. The stains he exposed were embarrassing.

"I've got some aspirin," he said.

He shook his head.

"You don't want me here."

"I didn't think you would want to be here," he said.

He moved his hand to his bosom. "This is soft. What makes it feel so real?"

"They are real," he said.

"What about below the waist?"

Toni reached for him and kissed him. His tongue forced its way in, probing his mouth. This was too strong, too determined, and too hard. He recoiled involuntarily. If he hadn't withdrawn, he might have gagged.

"I'm sorry, but I can't do this." David laughed nervously. "If you've got a penis and balls I'm going to throw up."

Toni slapped him. "I'm going to go." He paused at the door. "I'm not a joke."

"Then what are you?"

He closed the screen carefully – without a sound – and walked away. His heels crossed the courtyard, the spring on the door to the main building screeched and the door itself clacked loudly against some obstacle as it was flung aside. The echo of his footsteps stopped suddenly. Had he hesitated? Was he waiting inside for him to call after him? No, he told himself, he must have missed the faint click of the street entrance. The back door of the main building slammed, finalizing the silence.

Closing his eyes made him feel like he was spinning. The circling wasn't bad at first – just a slow round ride down toward sleep. When it grew faster he became frightened and then nauseous. He sat up and opened his eyes. The room had stopped, but he knew he was going to be sick. Jumping up, he stumbled out and hurried to the main building and the bathroom. He locked the door behind him before getting on his knees over the bowl. Nothing happened. He inhaled deeply and waited. Still nothing. After a moment, he flushed and watched the clear water swirl over the brown enamel. He was immune. His body obeyed and got to the sink. The face in the mirror wasn't his, but he would wash it and go back to bed.

He had a handkerchief, didn't he?

In searching his pockets he found Caroline's letter again. David paused and unfolded it carefully. The words swam on the page. Below her name were those 'O's and 'X's. He angrily wadded it up and threw it away, and then found the handkerchief. As he held the cloth under the faucet, he also soaked his bandaged finger before he realized what he was doing. Cursing, he tried wrapping the brace in his shirttail to absorb some of the moisture, but it didn't help much. That would have to do, he decided, he wasn't about to change it tonight. He wiped his face and reached for the latch on the door. Her letter had fallen between the toilet and the baseboard. Hidden beneath the shadow of the stool, the little paper ball could be easily overlooked – if that were possible. He hesitated. The paper had been painfully crumpled. And it seemed lost on the dismally dirty floor. He bent and picked it up, smoothed out her tortured handwriting, and stuck it back into his pocket.

The bathroom door hit the wall accidently when he opened it, making a loud noise which he was sure would wake everyone in the building. He waited for the sound of movement or an apartment door being cracked, but nothing happened. Only the bare bulb over the stairway had been disturbed. It was swinging back and forth, the shadows it cast from the stair railing and the pay phone on the wall were growing and shrinking with a strange silent pulse of their own. He stopped before the screen, and pressing his face close, peered out into the dark courtyard beyond. There wasn't a bright window to be found. Everyone was sleeping, dreaming their safe dreams in their safe beds. Except him. Even back home. He could imagine them wrapped in their blankets in their familiar places, transformed, like furniture, into dark shapes etched in the slate of night. What did he have to say to them? He had always been ignored. No one expected him to make noise. He picked up the telephone receiver breathlessly. His dime clinked down inside the machine and he dialed.

"I'd like to make this a collect call," he whispered. "...David Jacks."

He waited, trying not to listen to his own fearful thoughts.

"Hello. It's David, Mom. I'm sorry if I woke you up... They were at the bowling alley. They would play late, go for something to eat and then the twenty-minute drive back to the house. She was waiting up. ...That means his leg is all right... It was an accident, I didn't mean... I'm in New Orleans. ...You think I might come for a visit? I was going to be up near there this weekend... I see. ...Can't you – it was an accident... Wait. Please, can you tell me if Caroline is still at home. Is she ok? ...It was a simple question. Just say yes or no. ...Wait, will you?"

He hugged the receiver for a moment and then slammed it back into its cradle.

Chapter Five

David's father liked the sudden coldness of the kitchen tile beneath his feet in the morning. It belonged with beginnings, the fresh start of another new day. He always came quickly from his shower, shivering and blushing, wet hair slicked back and barefooted, to hesitate and then to tiptoe across to the stove for his first cup of steaming coffee. The floor could fool you to look at it. The summer sunlight on the clay-colored squares seemed a reflection of the warmth in the room: the hot stove, sausage popping in the fry pan, his wife in her housecoat and apron, and his over-sized oldest boy already at the table. But the floor was cold, even in the hottest summer. The shock made his beat-up feet feel fresh. When you got old, the little surprises of freshness were about all you could hope for.

Learning to tiptoe again hadn't been easy. The leg had taken months to heal and the knee had remained stiff and painful long after the stitches were out. His doctor had frowned the whole time. The man, nearly his own age and old enough to know better, kept telling him not to expect much – that if he was tough and worked hard he might be able to walk on the leg again. What the doctor hadn't known was that David's father was hardly the leathery stoic he appeared. Despite the balding head, the weathered face, and the sunburnt arms and neck, he was still a little boy inside, a little boy beating the bull to the gate. He was happy for the chance.

The accident had also given him the chance to slide out from beneath the earthen weight of the farm and his responsibilities as a father. David was gone – no word from him in three months. His oldest boy was running things without the least bit of guidance. And lying around the house, he had begun to talk to the woman he shared his life with, and had discovered the brittle sighs of her seclusion. She had a lot of reasons to blame him; what had happened was his own doing but, surprisingly, she didn't. It was almost as if she were blaming herself. Her only cross words were to tell him to stop being a baby and to get out from under foot.

With the coffee cup gingerly between his fingers, he carefully back stepped to let her get by. She pretended to ignore his smile and his Good Morning. He sat the cup at the head of the table and pulled out his straight-backed chair. His oldest, already eating, returned his hello with a glance up and a perfunctory half-smile from a full mouth. The boy was his mother's son all right. The hair and the eyes – and now that little smile. They were both so moody. It was enough to make you mad. David, at least, only smiled when he was pleased. His wife brought his breakfast: a well-laden plate of eggs, sausage and fried potatoes. He thanked her, but she didn't seem to hear. She joined them after a moment, and sat, wrapped tightly within her housecoat, poking at the lightly veiled yoke of her egg.

"You not feeling well?" he asked her.

"I'm all right," she said, with that same little half-smile. Her version made her seem shy and girlish. Almost as if she were afraid to mention the rest of whatever was on her mind. The smile was endearing, but he knew it didn't mean modesty. The deepening lines around her eyes and mouth were scarcely the worries of a blushing maiden. And she knew him too well. Whatever it was, he would have to wait until she finished picking at it. His own eggs were getting cold.

"David called last night," she said.

"Oh?" He swallowed.

"You two were so late coming back from the bowling alley. I thought I'd just wait till this morning."

"Where is he?" he asked.

"In New Orleans."

"He's in trouble?"

"Not that he said. He'd been drinking." She was looking at the back of the empty chair pulled tight against the tablecloth. "He wanted to know if he could come home."

"You told him he could?"

"I did not."

"Well...Well, maybe you should have told him he could."

"You ought to be mad at him," she said.

"Don't rightly know. Seems more to it then we figured. The Hawkins sure aren't telling why they didn't leave Caroline at that home they took her to."

She wanted to tell him why they had taken the girl away for a while, but then thought better of it. He didn't need to know.

"That girl isn't going to make any man a fit wife. I've watched Sally Hawkins suffer with her nearly twenty years. Why should I have it in my own house?"

"We should keep our own brand of suffering."

She dismissed him with a wave of her hand. Grimacing on the angry words he knew he shouldn't say, he started to count; and as it was such a habit, he calmed himself before reaching five. There wasn't any sense in arguing with her now, it would only make her dig in her heels that much more. The sore was too tender to touch. In another month, when the days were their hottest, and

David's birthday would get near, she'd remember those picnics for him by the river, and start to reconsider.

"I ran across that old tree house the kids built, when I was down fishing a couple of days ago," he said. "Decided I'd go up and take a look."

"You're lucky you didn't break your neck."

"Wasn't too bad. You should have seen the stuff up there. Somebody had lugged that old Texaco sign Dad had saved, down there from the barn." He glanced at his oldest boy, who shrugged in reply. "There were some mildewed books and the oddest collection of alphabet letters. Looked like they all came off different signs."

"He was teaching Caroline to read," his oldest said.

"That so."

He had guessed the collection was David's doing. When the boy was ten or eleven, his father had caught him nursing something under his jacket as they were riding back from town one Saturday. It was the letter 'I' from the front of the bank building. His punishment for stealing, a confession to the bank manager and extra chores for a week, had been accepted silently. At the time, his father had figured the theft to be just a childish prank. Now he could see how much more there was: years of caring about that little Hawkins girl. How many signs would it take to make an entire alphabet? You couldn't tell by looking at him, but the boy sure was the mastermind.

Chapter Six

There was that pounding again. David opened his eyes and squinted into the thick sunlight that was covering him. The dust particles seemed to swarm before him, obstructing his view. He held a hand to his forehead and glanced down. The blonde hair on his chest looked silver and strange. Where had he got to? Hadn't he gone to sleep in his own bed? The loud knocking at the door resumed. He bolted upright, his head throbbing. This was his room, after all. Then he remembered where he was supposed to be.

"Shit!"

Kicking his feet free from the tangled sheet, he jumped up and grabbed his jeans. He got to the door quickly. Outside were Martha and her granddaughter.

"God, I'm sorry," he said, holding the door for them. "I really wanted to get an early start. Hold on just a second and I'll be ready to go."

"No hurry. We've brought you breakfast," Martha said.

David looked up from his search for his shoes. Was she smiling at him? Her face was gray and exhausted, as if she hadn't slept at all. Something had happened.

"Are you all right?" he asked.

"I couldn't get to sleep last night. I guess I was too excited."

"You're not going to be sick?"

"Don't be silly. Why don't you come on outside and eat? It's a nice warm day. It still smells like paint in here."

"I haven't been here to open it up."

He followed them out to the courtyard.

"What time is it?" he asked, accepting the sack she had been holding. "Thanks."

"About eight-thirty. It's early yet."

David sat on one chair and pulled the lid from the coffee. It was steaming. In his half-awake, half-hungover state, her thoughtfulness seemed overwhelming. He was sorry he had ever thought badly of her. He took the plate from the bag, feeling a bit foolish, like a child unwrapping a birthday gift. Under the foil he found a hot slab of apple pie with cheese melted across the top.

"Pie?"

"You did like your pie," she said, smiling. She was rubbing her eyes.

"What?"

"Oh, I'm sorry. I've confused you with somebody else. Didn't you tell me you liked apple pie?"

"I never tried it for breakfast before."

"There's always a first time."

"You're in a good mood this morning," David said between mouthfuls.

"We get to fly away today. Like little birds."

"You need to get more sleep. You're funny," David said.

She laughed. In the bright sunlight, her face was alive and happy and young – much younger than he had imagined she might ever look. This was new and surprising. She had suddenly become someone whom he could be friends with. And he realized for the first time that he really didn't know her. Her laughter had been sharp and abrupt, as if there were another, more private, joke she was laughing at as well. He may not have deserved the laughter, but he was hard put to get annoyed about it. She had found him funny!

"I figured you would be mad at me for not showing up over there early," he said.

"Toni told me where you would be."

"Oh?"

"He was mad. I stopped him in the hall this morning. He acted like he didn't want to talk to me."

"He's probably not real happy this morning."

"You two should be friends. You're both such nice boys."

"He's not much of a boy."

"He is pretty. You could do the same thing if you wanted. Let your hair grow a little." She smiled mischievously.

"Not me. I like girls. I don't want to be one."

"It always seemed to me to be such a waste."

"Did you think I was like that?"

"Of course not," she said. "So what did you do to him?"

"Nothing."

"I thought maybe you hit him or something. He's always been like this. Hanging around and playing up to the normal men. He's been close to getting it a few times. Nobody would've held it against you if you had slugged him."

"I wouldn't hit him," David said.

"Of course you wouldn't want to. But I imagine it would be pretty hard to keep your temper with this thing standing close by, making eyes at you."

"He's not a thing –"

"You have to go potty, Missy?" she asked Lisa, who had been squirming. "Where's the restroom?"

"Inside the screen to your left."

"You don't have to defend him to me, Davey." She took her granddaughter's hand and led her toward the

73

door. "I know what he is. I'm surprised he didn't ask you for money as well."

The screen slammed after them.

"He asked me for love," David said quietly.

He wadded up the paper plate and sack and carried them into his room. The frayed floor was warm under his bare feet. He felt a spot of paint with his toe — part of the mess he had made a two nights before, now healed by the sunlight — and decided he would have to scrape and repaint. It didn't seem so much. The room was emptier than he thought. Even the ants had abandoned the beer can by the bed. There wasn't much to carry off. He could pack up for the two days he'd be gone and leave very little behind. The decent clothes he had left he took from the chifforobe and folded into a knapsack. Changing from his jeans into white corduroy pants, he traded what was in his pockets and took time to smooth out Caroline's letter again. The trash left from his breakfast was placed beside the empty can on the floor. The thought that someone might find it there, should he not return, with the ants searching out the last bits of apple pie, was somehow pleasing.

But he would be back. And in two days' time the humidity would turn the paper plate into something green. He carried his knapsack out and locked the door. Martha had already returned from the bathroom and was helping Lisa up on a chair in the courtyard.

"I don't see how you can stand to use that pigsty. It looks like somebody got sick in there last night," she said.

David reddened and then remembered that it hadn't been him.

"They clean it once a week."

He went to shower and shave. Returning shortly, his wet hair slicked back and his bare feet leaving tracks on the concrete, he hurriedly joined them to put on his shoes and socks. His head was pulsating.

"You sing real nice," Martha told him.

Had he been singing in the shower? He couldn't recall the last time he had wanted to.

"You could be a country-western singer easy," she said. "Maybe you should just stay in Nashville."

He stood up.

"You ready?"

"You going to leave all your furniture out here over the weekend?"

He nodded painfully. He would catch hell from the manager when he got back, but right now he didn't care. The stuff was junk anyway.

"Are you all right?" Martha asked.

"I think I'm beginning to sober up. I've got a headache."

"I don't have any aspirin," she said, but paused to look in her purse.

"It's ok." He motioned for them to leave.

"Everything I've got is packed."

"It's ok!"

"We can stop and get some."

He waved his hand as if he were brushing gnats from his face. As they left the building, Martha seemed to grow agitated and impatient. She snapped at the little girl for her slowness.

"You shouldn't be driving if you're sick," she finally said.

"If I was sick, I wouldn't go," he told her angrily.

He had to stop this, he told himself. She was just tired and worried. David paused and picked Lisa up so that they could walk faster. The little girl seemed lighter in the sunlight. She grasped the metal brace on his finger once again as if it were her own private handle.

"You're going to spoil her," Martha offered.

"You're already spoiled, aren't you?" he asked Lisa.

The little girl nodded, making Martha smile.

"You told Toni where you're going?" David asked.

"Why should I do that?"

"In case your daughter comes back."

"It's none of his business where I'm going," Martha said sharply. "I wish you hadn't brought her up. This isn't the day for sorrow."

"Sorry."

"You'd feel the same way I do, if you went through what I did."

"Sounds like she was trouble," David said.

"Who have you been talking to?"

"Oh, nobody. You've told me some of it."

"I wouldn't be surprised if half the building was gossiping about us. They're all a bunch of busybodies," Martha said. "It's been hell having to put up with their whispering. If I had only known."

"What's that?"

"George called me in Nashville and said they all had hepatitis and could I come down and help for two weeks until they got on their feet again. That was a year ago. You should have seen the way they were living. I didn't raise her to be white trash. No self-respecting woman would let her family go like she had."

"You get hepatitis from doing drugs, don't you?"

"She thought she was going to die from it. I swear I never knew anybody so bent on dying as she was. She had been warned not to drink after she got better. Hepatitis damages the liver. That didn't stop her. The last night she was here, she smelt like somebody had poured a bottle of whisky over her head." Martha looked at him. "That's what they told you about."

"I heard she was...er, seeing a lot of men."

"I wonder which little bird mentioned that."

"A few people said the same thing."

"Toni didn't tell you about the night George was killed?"

"No."

"Kathy and George had both gone out somewhere. I had gone to bed when I put Lisa down. About three in the morning someone starts leaning on the door buzzer to get in. I knew who it was all right, but I wasn't about to get out of bed. Kathy was always losing her keys. Then there's this big crash and wood splintering. Somebody had broken in the outside door. Then they start pounding on my apartment door. I'm about to have heart failure. I was afraid they'd break down mine too, so I get up and yell, asking who it is. It's Kathy all right. I opened the door and she shoves past like the devil is chasing her. There's some strange man with her. Probably somebody she picked up in a bar. Lisa is awake and crying. Her mother, her damn mother doesn't even hear her. She's running around the apartment, grabbing up her things. She was all sweaty and stinking, like she had run the whole way from some stinking barroom. This big guy is standing in the doorway, waiting for her. I tried to grab her, to make her stop, but she twists away and screams at me. 'George is dead!' she yells right there in front of Lisa. I couldn't see her face, she was standing between me and the door, but I knew she looked like a wild animal. I was afraid she'd kill me too."

"Jesus. What happened?"

"I went and held little Lisa until they left. There wasn't anything I could do. Then everybody comes down from upstairs to find out what's happened. That's why I figured you already knew about it. And then the police show up. They want to know about everything."

"Why did she do it?"

"Jealousy? I don't know. How can you tell what's going on in a crazy mind. Maybe she was just so drunk she didn't know what she was doing. Anyway, I decided then and there I'd have to protect myself, so I could take care of Lisa; she didn't have anybody else in the whole world. When the police saw me, I was looking pretty miserable. I figured if I was to keep looking miserable, they'd feel sorry for me, and maybe everybody else would too. It's worked real good."

"What?"

"You can laugh at me if you want, but I'm not stupid. You think that officer yesterday would have been so easy to talk to if he hadn't felt sorry."

"I never thought about it."

"Wait till we get to Nashville and I get some new things. I don't look half bad once I'm gussied up."

David stole a glance at her as they stopped at the corner. He had started to tell her that she wasn't unattractive, but something made him hesitate. She might be pretty if she fixed herself up, she might even be a knock-out. He didn't know much about it and he really didn't want to consider it. She made him nervous. Her eyes, which were warm and electric and almost dreamy with fatigue, were enough to draw him in. Already frightened by her gaze, he felt if she were to transform herself, he'd be hopelessly lost.

"You're all right," he heard himself say. He was reddening. She must have noticed for she beamed at him.

"You sure you don't want to stop for aspirin?"

He shook his head.

"Will I be glad to be free of this place," she said.

They were crossing Bourbon Street, which was empty and exhausted in the morning sun. Plastic trash bags were lined up along the curb. Water gushed from a bar's open doors on the corner and, after a moment, a man with a hose appeared, to wash the steps as well. David noticed for the first time how the buildings, above the storefronts and dead neon and the girdles of ironwork balconies, were brightly colored like the cottages in an alpine village. He could almost imagine the little fat men in the funny hats. Martha took his arm. Before them, a girl was sleeping in a doorway, her bare leg stretched out across the narrow sidewalk. As they stepped around her, Martha tapped her lifeless tennis shoe and the girl shuddered.

"Still alive." Martha smiled at him as if it was a joke he was taking part in.

"How did you end up here?" she asked. "I recall you said something about a fight with your family."

"They didn't want me to see a girl. They thought she was retarded."

"Was she?"

"I don't know what to think anymore."

"Did you love her?"

"Didn't I already tell you about it?"

"I don't recall if you did or not. It must've been your first time."

"Why do you say that?" he asked surprised.

"You seem real hurt. The first time always hurts the worst."

"I blew it."

"Somebody else will come along."

"I blew it, damn it. I ran away!"

"You're not a bad person, Davey. If you just open up your heart you'll find that things will get better."

"Things can't get much better, I'm so happy," he murmured.

"Look at me, Davey. I opened up my heart to you and look what's happening. I'm getting out of this horrible place. There's nothing that says you have to run away again."

"Maybe it was for the best."

"There you go. Just think about what you would've missed if you hadn't shown up on my doorstep."

David snorted.

"Well, you know what I mean," she said. "You know, you should get out for good, while you can. This city's like a great queen whore who wrecks men. You end up in tears."

If it were night, David would have agreed with her, but the daylight made these streets easier. There was a quiet here he hadn't known at home, there were no expectations. Everyone moved under the weight of the humidity. Passions wilted with the slow afternoons. At the

79

next corner, there was the small street running on to Decatur Street and the levee. A low wall of black clouds sat in the southern sky.

"What do you know," Martha said. "It looks like it's going to rain."

"Everybody's said it's supposed to rain every afternoon this time of year."

"It poured for two days straight right before you showed up," Martha said. "That was when George died."

"People die in the rain around these parts?" David asked.

"George..."

David looked at her.

"What?" she asked.

"You were going to say something about George."

She seemed distracted and perplexed. After a moment, she shrugged her shoulders.

"I must be tired," she said.

"The car's right here."

As they crossed the lot, David noticed that the trailer seemed to be leaning forward, drawing the rear of the car down under its weight. He would have to be careful not to drag the hitch in ruts. That dresser probably shouldn't have been put in first. David put Lisa down. For a moment, when he bent over, the nausea and throbbing behind his eyes came back sharply and he thought he might get sick right there, but it passed. Martha handed him the keys and squeezed his hand.

"Are we ready?" she asked happily, leading the little girl around to the passenger's side.

David just shook his head as they climbed in.

Naturally, the car wouldn't start right away. He pumped the gas pedal gingerly and tried again. When the engine finally turned over, he nursed it up to an idle and let it sit for such a long time that Martha looked up at him. She had been getting Lisa settled with crayons and a coloring book. He put a finger to his lips, then smiled and put it in gear. They were off. He rolled the car carefully out into the street without the slightest scraping and drove back across the French Quarter. The car seemed to be running fine, until it stalled at the first stoplight.

"What's wrong?" Martha asked angrily.

"It must not be warmed up yet."

The engine turned over easily and they turned out onto an empty Rampart Street.

"Shouldn't we stop and have it checked?" she asked.

"It'll be all right once we're out on the highway."

The car died again when they were stopped at Canal.

"You said the car was ok."

"The idle must be too low, is all."

"We should have it fixed," she said.

"Sure, if you want to waste the morning looking for a station that's open and that'll do it." The engine turned over as he spoke. "So we're going on?"

"If you think," she said.

As they waited at the next light, he gunned the engine so that it wouldn't happen again.

The light went green and they barreled down the empty street, following the girder work of the highway past warehouses and the gingerbread storefronts grown gray with dust. The trailer bounced across the potholes. In the overpass shadow, the air, which had begun brightly, now seemed threatened, almost translucent with impending gloom. The world had cooled. They found the ramp and shot up beyond the rooftops and above the trees. The sky widened before them like a flower blossoming suddenly. There was the city, a few shining towers, the Superdome half-completed eggshell and the stooped roofs of all the crowded houses huddled in the gleaming scythe of the river. The wall of the storm was swelling forward from the south. The fine fiber beneath its rolling belly meant rain already falling, but they were racing away.

All the small flat streets, the lush back gardens, the front stoops and all the gaping screens grew insignificant and hidden.

"Am I glad to be free from that place," Martha said. Her arm was resting on the back of the seat, her hand behind his shoulder. "You want your neck rubbed? It would help your headache."

"That's all right."

"If it hadn't been for George and this one, I wouldn't have gone. I'm just not used to living like this. Did I tell you my Daddy was a Presbyterian minister in Nashville? I was raised in the Church. Not one of those boys at the dances would dare lay a hand on the preacher's daughter. Not that I didn't want them to, mind you." She laughed. "You know what George did after he got back on his feet? He took us all dancing. I hadn't danced in years." She bent over the little girl. "That's a cow. You know what a cow says?"

Lisa shook her head.

"The cow says moo," David said.

"Moo?" she repeated.

"Do you like to dance?" Martha asked him.

"Not really. I never learned how."

Lisa held up a picture of a chicken for David to see.

"That's a hen. She goes cluck, cluck." David checked his enthusiasm. His head hurt when he moved it too quickly.

"It's easy to learn. I could show you a few steps some time," Martha said.

"I'm going to have to turn around and come straight back."

The little girl flipped the pages and held up another for him.

"Don't go disturbing David while he's driving," Martha told her.

"That's all right," he said. "That's a pig. He goes oink, oink. Can you say that?"

"Oink, oink."

"Somebody's not given you the proper education," he said.

"Her father was real good with her, but he never seemed to have much time," Martha said. "She certainly needs a man around. Since you've been helping us these last two days she's been a real angel."

"What was George like?" David asked.

"He could do anything he turned his hand to. It seemed like he had talent for everything he tried. Before he hooked up with my daughter he had been a mechanic for those race car drivers. He used to follow them around the country. He was always talking about places like Indianapolis and Daytona. That was his first love, I think. It was a shame he gave it up."

"Someone said he was handsome."

"Somebody told you that you look like him," she said with a knowing grin.

"Toni thought I was his brother."

"He wasn't what you'd call gorgeous. He looked like you."

"I was just asking."

"I'm teasing you," she said. "Women got real weak-kneed around him. He was nice to look at. And he was one of the few men I've known that really understood women. That made it worse. If you've ever been around a woman who made your insides into wet noodles, you'd know what I mean."

"I don't know."

"You sure?"

He avoided her look. She knew.

"Toni always said he knew what it felt like," she laughed. "It was two or three times a day with him. Maybe you have to be a woman to understand. Or almost a woman. George was something all right."

As the few cars on the highway slowed on the incline of the bridge over the Industrial Canal, David smiled to himself, imagining what it would be like to have women get weak knees around him. He braked before a semi. Part of leaving home was envisioning your return. He had seen himself going back one day, a much older and wiser man. In denim, with a face aged by sun and sorrow, he would step from his jeep and talk softly. They would be awed into silence. All the young girls would swoon. The truck ahead had reached the peak of the bridge. As they started their rush down, David pulled out to pass. The huge tires were soon rolling by and roaring outside Martha's window. They would know what he had come for, and would step aside when he looked toward her parents' house. He would start walking alone across the field. Could he really expect her to still be there — waiting? Life could have gone on in the time he would be gone. She might have been put away, and become a disheveled zombie let out to sit in the grass in the afternoon. Or she might have escaped that and married. Was he to look in bewilderment at the child holding her hand? He gunned past the semi's cab and rushed down, back to the wide expanse of flat land below. To become somebody like George, he would have to take more chances. Working at a print shop and living in a dirty room wasn't going to do it. This trip was going to be a start — a new way of living. They were free from the traffic once more. The highway stretched open before him, an easy aisle through the suburb tract houses.

They had escaped the rain as well; the dark clouds were behind them and growing smaller. Soon, the houses and new streets bordering the highway became scattered and were replaced by patches of lush green grass and trees that reminded him of cotton candy. The sky out here was blank and blue, as calm as the sky he had found in the city the day of the hurricane scare. Everyone had urged him to tape up his windows and hoard jugs of tap water. He couldn't quite believe their seriousness. That afternoon had seemed quieter than any he had known. It hadn't even rained. This wasn't like home, where the storm would come rumbling over the hills and blot out the sun and the last bit of blue before the first drops would fall in large sloppy splotches. There was too much sky here to fill, you were on the rim of an abyss too vacant and too serene to understand, let alone predict.

Being out here did beat being in the box that was the city. He hadn't realized how much he had missed the open fields. Despite his headache and the stiffness in his legs, the nice day was cheering him up. There was a cool wind now. The bushes and trees on the left side of the highway had dissolved into a broad low bay as unbroken and as blue as the sky. A tiny white sail floated in the horizon haze. The trailer was bucking in the wind, but it wasn't anything serious. If the trip was going to be as easy as this, he would glide into Nashville rejuvenated. Even Martha seemed to be sharing how he felt, she certainly wasn't the grouch he had expected.

She had stood Lisa up in the space between them and was digging into a sack behind the seat.

"Are you hungry?" she asked. "We brought this over before we came to get you."

The smell of fried chicken engulfed him, turning his stomach. His head throbbed in unison with the nausea. All he could manage, without opening his mouth to give in to the sickening urge, was strongly shaking his head. Martha handed a drumstick to the little girl. He quickly rolled down his window all the way, so that the rush of air would dispel the odor and mask the sound of their eating. It seemed to be working.

Another sound came in with the wind from the window. Faint at first, the siren then grew louder and louder until it was almost on top of him. He thought it might be an ambulance and slowed. A highway patrol car appeared in his rearview mirror, tailing him closely. As he braked and hesitated to pull off because of the bucking of the trailer, the patrol car's loudspeaker ordered him to the shoulder. His tires were sliding in the loose gravel. He fought the wheel for control and brought the car to a safe stop. The siren became silent. The cop in his mirror climbed out and walked toward them.

"What's going on?" Martha asked through a mouthful of chicken.

"The highway patrol."

They looked at each other nervously. "Jesus. Were you speeding?"

Before he could answer the patrolman was at his window.

"Please step out of the car."

David got out. Martha leaned past Lisa to stare up at the cop from the open door.

"What's the matter, Officer?" she asked.

"You've got a front heavy trailer, ma'am. The first strong wind gush and you'll be off the highway."

"David!"

"I noticed the bucking," he told the patrolman. "But it wasn't making the car hard to handle."

"It isn't safe to drive it this way. You're entering the causeway up ahead where the wind is stronger. You'll have to redistribute the weight."

"I'll have to unload the whole trailer."

"I can't let you go on with it like this."

"David, I swear," Martha said. "You'd think you were trying to kill us all."

"I didn't plan this."

"Well, son," the patrolman said.

"Christ." David slammed his door in frustration and stormed back to the trailer.

When he pulled the lock off and yanked the doors open, two smaller boxes fell out at his feet. The short drive had settled the odds and ends in a tangle. Removing one more piece might bring everything down on his head. He tried to figure out what to grab first. One large box in the corner seemed to be a safe bet – nothing was resting on it. He tugged and got it free. The flaps of the top were splattered with drops of his sweat by the time it was settled on the gravel. The patrolman ambled back and stood beside him as he tried to catch his breath.

"You don't look so good, son."

"I'm sick."

"You're better off sick than dead."

He went to lean against his patrol car hood. David wanted to curse him, but he lowered his head and forced himself to pull another box from the trailer. This one split apart just as he was about to sit it down. Lisa's toys tumbled out across the white stones.

He was ready to cry. Bending carefully, his head throbbing and the brace on his finger making his hand clumsy, he began to gather up the contents. The toys weren't much: a doll with a broken arm, some dirty doll clothes and an incomplete tea set. The rest, like the plastic egg that pantyhose came in and the oversized empty spool, had become toys out of default. Her childhood suddenly seemed to be worth very little. He heard a car door slam in front of the trailer and was certain it was Martha coming back to stick her nose in. After a moment, Lisa appeared with her coloring book. She was alone. David leaned forward to look past her. There wasn't a sign of her grandmother.

"Martha!" he shouted.

No answer. Lisa began to help him pick up the toys.

"I'll keep an eye on her for you," the patrolman said above him. "What's her name?"

"Lisa."

"Come on over here, Lisa. Out of your Daddy's way."

David motioned for her to go with him. The cop picked her up and carried her back to the hood of his patrol car. David was on his feet with a hand over his mouth.

"Excuse me."

He rushed down the embankment and knelt beside a bush and began to throw up.

"Your Daddy's not feeling too well," the patrolman said when Lisa looked after him.

"He's not my Daddy. He's David from upstairs."

"Where are your parents?"

"I don't know."

The patrolman scratched his nose and moved Lisa back from the edge of the hood after feeling the metal to make sure it wasn't going to be too hot. When David started to climb up to the shoulder again, the cop was waiting above him.

"Sorry," David told him.

"Where are the girl's parents?"

"Her father's dead. I don't know where the mother is."

"Why do you have her?"

"The woman in the car is her grandmother. I'm just doing them a favor."

"She has proof of custody?"

"I don't know," David turned. "Martha!"

The car door slammed again. Her footsteps crunched lightly across the gravel. David was suddenly apprehensive. Why did her walk sound different? Then she appeared beside the trailer open door. She had changed her clothes and was wearing high heels. The faded dress was gone, replaced by a light silky-looking blouse and dungarees. Her auburn hair, which he had never seen, was loose and fluffed out about her face and neck. Her face was made up. She smiled from her darkened eyes, noticeably excited and a little embarrassed. Was she flushed? David gaped at her, trying to discern the woman he had known. Only the eyes were similar. Nothing else remained. He didn't know what to say. The patrolman seemed to be confused as well. He looked from her to David and then back at her again.

"With all this moving, I didn't get a chance to clean up till now," she told him sweetly.

"The boy says this is your granddaughter."

"Yes."

"You've got legal custody of her?"

"Not from a court."

"Where's her mother?"

"We're taking her to Tennessee where her mother is going to meet us."

"I was told that you didn't know where her mother is."

"I suppose I forgot to mention it to David."

"You're going to have to provide me with some identification that proves who you are and who she is."

"What for?" Martha asked.

"For all I know you two could be kidnappers."

"Just ask her. She'll tell you I'm her grandmother."

"Identification."

"This is plain crazy," Martha said. "You don't have anything better to do than bother normal folks?"

"I could take you in to the office and impound your vehicle."

"For Christ's sake, if you've got anything at all, show it to him," David told her. "I've got to be back at work Monday."

"Well, I've got her birth certificate in one of these boxes. Will that be enough?"

The patrolman nodded.

David helped her look through the boxes he had already unloaded. As they bent over the last one, he found himself staring at her cleavage. A bit of her bra was exposed. The cream-colored lace on her white skin made him forget why they were searching. She caught him and smiled.

"It must still be in the trailer," she said.

She went to peer into the jumble and spotted the box she thought contained her papers. He dug it out. Opening the box seemed to be too much for her, her fingers fluttered, somehow suddenly genteel, and despite his disbelief he was quickly helping her. When she bent over once more her small waist and round hips were smartly

89

defined. He couldn't understand why he hadn't noticed her body before.

Her glance up at them gave away her pleasure in being watched.

"Here's the birth certificate," she said, handing it to the patrolman. She continued looking. "She has my last name. Kids now days don't seem to think getting married is very important. Here's my daughter's high school diploma."

She found a photo album and stood up to open it for him.

"This is all of us. That's me with Lisa's father. There's her mother."

The patrolman examined the photos, eyed David, and then looked back at the album.

"You related to the girl's father?" he asked.

"Stepbrother," David replied.

Martha stared at him. The patrolman handed the papers back to her.

"I apologize for the inconvenience. With all this business of missing kids these days, I've got to be suspicious if I'm to do my job."

"That's all right. If she were kidnapped, I'd want you to be asking the same questions. Are we done?"

He nodded. Martha gave the album and papers to David and went to get the little girl.

"I appreciate you keeping an eye on her while I changed," she said. "You must have kids of your own."

"Two."

"Boys I bet."

"As a matter of fact —"

"Well, Lisa and I will go wait in the car. It's awful hot out here."

David glanced up from the album to watch her lead the little girl away. He had been leafing through the pages, looking for George. The know-it-all smirk he had worn in the framed portrait wasn't here. Without it he seemed just average. The photos were typical enough: George in a t-shirt on a blanket in the sun, or George holding the baby. Nothing to explain how he demanded such affection.

"You feeling better, son?" the patrolman asked.

"Yeah. It must have been something I ate."

David put the album back in the box. He was telling the truth. His nausea was gone and the headache had lessened.

"The cross wind has died down some," the patrolman said, scratching his nose again.

"Yes sir, it has."

"If you're careful, you might not have any trouble. You would pull over if it started bouncing?"

"Sure."

"I'm going to let you go, on the condition you redistribute the weight when you stop tonight. Can I trust you to do that?"

"Yes sir."

"It's for their safety."

"I promise."

"Be careful."

The patrolman returned to his car and pulled out. They waved to each other. He was gone before David could raise his arm to wave a second time. Wiping the sweat from his forehead, David began throwing the boxes back into the trailer.

Chapter Seven

By the time they reached the far side of Lake Pontchartrain, David was weary. The wind rising from the vast water had constantly buffeted them. The car and trailer had become unwieldly and stubborn like a muley cow protecting its wayward calf. He had to muscle it most of the way. This swamp before Slidell was a relief, there were a few pines to break the breeze and the tall grass looked easy to lie in, although he knew solid footing wasn't to be found there. Water, laid bare in random patches, offered its mystery of depth as a slate smeared and forgotten. Relaxing back into a calm highway was making him drowsy.

The pavement seemed endless without hills or curves to interrupt his steady hold on the steering wheel. He leaned forward awhile and then stretched lazily.

"Do you think the radio might wake Lisa up?" he asked. He still couldn't bring himself to look at the woman next to him. She was a stranger. He didn't know if he would laugh or be frightened by what he saw.

"Yes," Martha said. "She was real excited last night. It took me forever to get her to sleep."

"You want to check the map and see how far it is to 59?"

He heard the paper rustle.

"We're not very far away at all," she said.

When he glanced over, he found her closer than he had expected. She was holding up the map for him. Avoiding her face was impossible. He turned back to the road, feeling like a child who has just been caught playing with himself.

"Thanks," he mumbled, hoping the new highway might provide some distraction.

"Don't be afraid of me, Davey. I'm the same person."

"I'm not afraid of you. Why would you say that?"

"You've been acting odd ever since you got back in the car."

"Well, you do look different."

"For the better I hope."

"Yes."

"I didn't realize it would be such a shock for you. These last few months have been so much work, that I never had a chance to clean myself up. I guess I've been pretty depressed about my situation."

"How old are you anyway?"

"I'm forty-five."

He didn't know if he should believe her.

"A guy at work was ribbing me about running off with a forty-year-old sexpot. I didn't think that was what I was doing."

"You can go back and tell him that I wasn't so much to look at when you started, but I got better the farther you went."

"I will not."

"You're such a prude."

"I am not," he said, getting annoyed.

"There's nothing wrong with being a prude. I'm one myself at times." She reached into the back seat to pull the blanket up on Lisa. "I sure got in a land of trouble with that apartment building owner 'cause I wouldn't let any old men bring their girlfriends in."

"That was the reason I moved out."

"You should have said something to me. I would have made an exception."

"That's not what you said when I first came."

"I didn't know you yet, Davey. I made that rule because those girlfriends the old men had weren't nothing but hookers. Everybody would think the building was a whorehouse. You wouldn't have wanted to rent a room there if it had looked like that sort of place."

"Want to bet?"

"You can't fool me," she said.

They had reached the turn off for the other highway. David took the ramp and eased on to the new road going north.

"Actually," Martha said. "The place was looking better by the time you came, though some of it was hopeless. I had cleaned for two months straight."

"Did you notice that smell like there was something rotting?" David asked.

"The woman who owned the place." Martha giggled. "She was as big and sweaty as a side of beef. And old enough to have gone bad. She'd come to call and take fifteen minutes just to get up the front steps. She'd climb one step, stop to rest and then take another one. It had been ten years since she'd been upstairs in her own building. She would always come straight in and plop down in the divan by the window. Her chins would wobble around like she was giving the apartment the once-over, you know – checking me out – but it was really George that she was looking for. She'd act real sweet if he wasn't there. Always talking George this and George that, as if they were in tight with each other and I should be happy that she was telling me about him. As if I was a stranger. When George was there, she would make up some stupid errand for me to run so she could be alone with him. I hated to hear her panting up those front steps. That divan began to stink from her sitting on it. She smelled evil.

"I swear the woman thought she had a secret deal going on with David. Maybe she did. Every time I would try to talk to him about the way she was acting, he would just laugh and tell me it was my imagination."

"You mean George," David interrupted.

"What did I say?"

"You said my name."

"Oh, how silly. I must be tired. Well, you know how she was. If she had her way, I'd be run so ragged from cleaning and running errands that I wouldn't have had time to take care of my own. Then she could have you all to herself. As if you wanted to have anything to do with her anyway."

"You're dreaming with your eyes open," David said. "I don't know the woman."

"What? Oh... I must be falling asleep. What was I saying? I've forgotten what I was talking about."

"The woman who owned the building."

"It's so hard to sleep sometimes. I have such dreams. Usually I try to lay down with Lisa when she takes her nap, it's easier in the light. That building has made me afraid to close my eyes."

"You can sleep now," David said.

"No, I'm all right. Really. Besides, you need some company."

"I might fall asleep you mean."

"I didn't say that, Davey."

"I'll need somebody to talk to later on, like tonight."

"I don't want to dream about George and that woman after talking about them. You don't understand how horrible it was." Her hand wiped at her face. "The police took me down to identify George after the accident. They had found him all sprawled out in an alley over near St. Charles, behind a bar: The Blue Rooster."

"That's a gay bar."

"You can just put that out of your mind right now! George wasn't that way and I don't want to hear another word. Toni was always spreading stupid stories. He wanted to pretend George was interested in him!

"The only reason he was out that night at all was Kathy put him up to pimping for her. I tried to protect him from those women. He wasn't like what they thought he was. He was too attractive for his own good. He'd smile from politeness and they'd think he was seducing them. I just didn't try hard enough," her voice cracked. "I had to take Lisa along with me to the police station. There wasn't anyone to babysit. They had a girl watch her while they took me back. She was so frightened. What could I tell her? They took me to this big cold room and showed me the..." She was crying. "He... he was all bloated up. His face was bruised so badly. And his hips and legs were all twisted up and crushed..."

"Hey," David said softly.

"Why him? Why? He was so young, Davey. He wouldn't have hurt a fly. He was mine, just as much if I had him myself. It was so hard to take... so hard alone..."

David wanted to reach out a hand to comfort her, to say something to ease the tears he could only glimpse from the corner of his eye, but he didn't know what would help.

"It's rough losing somebody you love," he said.

That sounded stupid.

"I'm all right. You pay attention to the road. I've got no call to distract you."

He patted her shoulder and before he could withdraw she was squeezing his hand.

"Thank you," she said.

His hand returning to the wheel was clumsy and wooden. It hadn't meant much.

"You're kind deep down, you know that?" she said. "You're the first real friend I've had in ages. I don't know what guardian angel sent you along to me, but I'm grateful.

Being in that city was like being in jail. There wasn't anybody to talk to. I thought the old woman would sympathize with me for losing George. We hadn't been close, but we had been friendly. She wouldn't give me the time of day except to nitpick and think up new things for me to do. She blamed me for George dying! She wouldn't sit any more when she came, she wouldn't even look at me! She'd just put out her big fat hand for the rent money. Then she'd repeat every complaint those men had. As if I wasn't already working myself to death. You know what the rest of them are like. I was in a nuthouse full of nuts! I was so afraid I'd end up like them. I could feel the evil and crazy thoughts slipping in. My skin began to feel slimy, I swear to God. Lisa and I prayed every night – it was all we had left."

"You think it worked?" David asked.

"What have I been saying?"

She glanced back at Lisa again.

"It was for her sake. Praying won't work unless it's for somebody else. I had to get her away from there. She couldn't understand what had happened to her parents. I'm sure she thinks they're gone because she's been bad. She has nightmares. And mixed up! She says the oddest things. When you showed up she told me that you looked different. God only knows what thoughts she's having. Every now and then the carefree little girl I used to have will come out, but it's not too often. She was touched by the evil the most."

"She seems all right to me," David said.

"She used to talk, Davey."

"Didn't we all."

"You told me that where you come from folks didn't speak much. That you weren't used to it."

"I don't remember," he said. He vaguely recalled saying that one night when he was tired and wanted to get away from her.

"Why are you so quick to deny everything?"

"I... I don't know what you mean."

"Every time I say something about you, you tell me I'm mistaken. How am I supposed to trust you if you're not fessing up?"

"I don't know. I hadn't thought about it."

"Well, think about it. It's real annoying."

What he had said about his family was true: they had rarely spoken and then only when there was no other way out. But he did remember talking, spilling his guts and dreams, and discussing all the small items of childhood. To Caroline. Couldn't she see that was what he meant?

One minute she was saying how much she liked him and the next she was picking on him. Maybe she was right. If he had been acting the way she said, he certainly hadn't known it. Maybe all this time he had been trying to get her to stop liking him. This was too much to think about. He lit a cigarette and glanced away from the rolling highway. The road was bordered on both sides by thick groves of tall pine. Occasionally an impression of blue-gray from the other lane or the sun-brightened green field would weave through the brown trunks and dark needles like a mutant thread in the thick undergrowth.

"Another one?" she asked. "You just had one a few minutes ago."

He looked at his cigarette and rolled down his window a bit more without answering. Did she want him cold and mean? This talk was going to make him that way real quick.

"Where I come from you either take a person or you leave them," he said.

"Folks shouldn't compromise at all?"

"I didn't say that." He tossed the cigarette out the window.

"You didn't have to do that. I was worried about how much you've been smoking. It's not good for you, you know."

"You don't have to worry about me."

"I can't help myself, I guess," she said. "You know, Davey, when you showed up on my doorstep you looked as if you had just lost your only friend in the world."

"Maybe I did."

"You don't have to be alone. There are other folks that care about you. I do."

"You may be the only one."

"You don't have much to keep you in New Orleans. Why don't you stay with us in Nashville awhile? You could nose around for a couple weeks and see if you'd like it."

"I don't have the money."

"You can't eat that much. You can be my guest. I could even loan you a little for cigarettes when you needed."

"I've got a job in New Orleans."

"Just think about it. Let me know when we get there. It might do you a world of good. A body gets awful lonesome being out on their own all alone."

"What do you want in return?" he asked.

"What on earth did your family do to you?"

He couldn't bring himself to answer her. How was he to explain what had happened? It seemed as convoluted as those skeins of yarn his mother would hand him to untangle when he was a child. Without a beginning or an end, it was hopeless. Caroline had always been there — from the time they played together below the porch swing where their mothers snapped beans, to the morning he left — she was wound about his life. He had tried to free himself when he was eleven — you were a sissy to play with girls then — but her blossoming sensuality soon became a new and compelling tie. She was his twin, his sister, his lover. What was between them was too large and too intertwined to unravel. And talking about it would betray her.

He had to smile in remembering the small betrayal of childhood: the year he wouldn't have anything to do with her. He had been brutal. When she followed him, he screamed at her. If she offered a game or a shared treat he would scoff and run away. It wasn't the problem with her eyes that embarrassed him. He would never make fun of her over that. Never. It was because she was a girl. Boys didn't play with girls. At least those boys he hung out with. Despite his willingness, at her expense, to be part of the crowd, their acceptance hadn't been easily gained. In the beginning he wasn't very good at sports and it was some time before he escaped being the last one picked for teams. And he soon found that he missed the imaginary worlds Caroline and he had created and lived in. By the time he realized his mistake, he had dug himself into a deep hole. She rebuffed his attempts to make up. His exile might have been final if he hadn't offered to help her with her reading. Even now she would tease him about going off to play with the boys rather than admit her gratitude.

The eleven-year-old deserved his lumps. Stalking crows across the side yard with his brother's BB gun in the summer afternoon, he had become the center of the universe. No one could touch him, or so he thought. When the screen slammed he swung to take aim on the intruder. His mother appeared from the house and frowned. That was enough to make him lower the rifle. Her plain long face, similar to his own, had those warning lines at the edges of her mouth which perpetually suggested that a frown was about to form. An actual frown meant business. She walked out into the tall grass.

"Caroline's mother just called. She wants to know if you'll go fetch her from the tree house."

"No, Ma'am."

"What do you mean no?"

"I'm killing crows."

"The crows will be there tomorrow." She examined him oddly. "Come on, I'll go with you."

This was different. His mother had never gone for a walk with him before. She was a town girl. She didn't care for the mess of the cow pastures. David followed her down from the house willingly, curious as to what she would say and do and at the same time self-conscious. It seemed like a good chance for a serious talk. Was there something he had done wrong?

Whatever it was, she didn't seem to be in a hurry to say it. They went the long way around the little village of car chassis — she wouldn't let them play there in summer because she thought the high weeds were a haven for snakes — and joined the tractor trail running back under the clumped oaks at the bottom of the hill. Beyond the trees the trail climbed up again into the tall hay in the first pasture. He went as the intrepid hunter on safari, dragging his feet in the tractor rut dust, and aiming listlessly at the birds on wing. He dared not fire. The damn American woman who had hired him needed his protection and he had to save his ammo. The natives were about to flush the man-eater from the hay.

"She wasn't sure if Caroline's brother stayed down there with her," his mother was saying. "She knew Caroline wouldn't come back on her own."

"She's afraid of the cows," he replied. Was that all?

They had reached the top of the rise.

"David, I've been meaning to talk to you for some time. You're old enough to be told. You've already started to change. I've been finding stains on your sheets."

"It was an accident."

"You'll have to settle that with your own conscience. You need to know what it means. You've probably heard it at school from those boys you play with."

"No, Ma'am."

"Well, you've noticed that girls are different?"

He nodded his head.

"Girls have different private parts too. They're the opposite of yours. When a man and woman fall in love and get married, there's a physical side to it. Yours gets hard and it's put inside the woman's. That's how a woman gets pregnant. When the time comes for you, when you're

101

truly in love with the girl, it will be very simple and you'll understand much better than I can explain. Does this make sense to you?"

"I think so." David wasn't sure how he was supposed to feel about this revelation. He had wondered what the other kids had been joking about. At least now, he wouldn't have to pretend he knew.

"The physical part is real easy for a man, but it's not for a woman. That's the part I want you to understand. So many men don't. A woman falls in love with a man because he's earned her trust. You go after her and win her and she gives the most precious thing she has to give: the physical part of love. It's not to be taken lightly. Some men think it's all a contest – they're trying to get more than their buddies have gotten. You're not to do that ever, you understand?"

He nodded again, solemnly.

"Is there anything you want to ask me?"

David looked at her and then looked away at a lone sparrow flying across the open sky. He wanted to ask questions, but he didn't have the questions to ask. He suddenly thought of what a boy had told him: that a girl at school wiggled when she walked because she had shit in her pants. It sounded stupid at the time. She would laugh if he asked that now. And the girl's wiggle didn't seem connected to what they were talking about. She was still expecting a question.

"You and Dad... that's what you guys do?"

Her lips knitted tighter about the frown she had been holding back since they left the house.

"You're here, aren't you?"

David wanted to escape this discussion.

"I think I understand."

"Well, you come and ask if you need to know anything else."

They had reached the gate to the cow pasture. David ran ahead to unlatch it and instead of his usual ride, swinging the gate out wide with his weight, he merely held it for her. The wooden crossbeams suddenly seemed too flimsy to support him.

Once the gate was latched, he was off ahead of her again. The tractor trail emerged from the clump of trees surrounding the gate and turned to run across the top of a rich and swelling slope. Below him, as he ran with gun in hand, were a few cows grazing near the small shade tree, further down the highway and still further, beyond the hazy hills of deep summer, the outward arc of the Ohio lay across the green like a discarded ribbon from the unwrapped sky. This was his.

"David!" she was calling.

She was walking slowly, trying to avoid the cow paddies. He stopped running, but continued on to the top where the trail ended in a turnaround and a large mound of earth that only now, after a year, had begun to sprout weeds. A cow looked on as he climbed to the top to await her. Behind him, a footpath led back into the woods and down a steep hill. At the bottom was a cool green valley with a running brook and leaves so thick that light there was green and hushed in a way to make whispers inaudible. Voices hadn't touched it.

He had built a tree house there.

And in his stupidity, he had shared it with Caroline. She had seemed a safe bet, at first she would only come into the pasture if he was with her. Because of her eyes, she would turn and suddenly be face to face with a cow that hadn't been there a moment before. If she dawdled, the cattle coming for a look would seem to be jumping out all around her. Seeing them that way would scare anyone. He had banked too much on her fear and had forgotten that she loved the spot more than he did. She was soon talking her brother into bringing her. Then her brother's friends. Little was left of what he wanted. And now this: his mother's intrusion. She was traipsing up the last hill into the turnaround.

"It's pretty steep down to the tree house," he said when she reached him. "You want me to go and bring her up?"

"No. I want to see if you all should be playing down here in the first place."

He slid down from the mound angrily and led her to the footpath. So let them tear it down and scatter the boards, he thought. He didn't care anymore.

They descended the slope slowly, the path was narrow and uneven and branches had to be held back so that they could get through. He was also taking his time in the hope she would get discouraged and turn back. He knew what she would say when she saw it. Ahead was a small cleared space atop a large rock before the final climb down. The tree house couldn't be seen yet so he paused there to let her catch her breath.

"How much further?" she asked.

"There's still a ways to go."

It was then they heard the rustling and the tearing at branches below. Caroline appeared, her hair tangled and in her face, her arms flaying at the foliage and her new breasts jiggling as she struggled in her rush up the hill. David started to laugh at her and turned to share the chuckle with his mother. The anxiety on her face made him stop short. Something was wrong.

"Help!" Caroline cried to them.

They hurried to her.

By sliding down the leafy embankment, David reached her first. She grabbed his hand as if she were drowning. Her face was sweaty and tear-stained.

"Michael fell out of the tree. He's broken his legs!"

"Just now?"

"A long time ago."

"Why didn't you come get us?" he demanded.

His mother made it to them.

"Help, please," Caroline turned to her, discarding his hand. "Michael can't get up!"

"Why didn't you come and get us?" David asked again, angrily. "Are you stupid?"

"Shut up!" his mother ordered. "Run and get the men. They're across the highway. Now!"

Her 'shut up' was a slap to his face. Red with shame, he started back up, scrambling quickly to the top.

Throwing the rifle high on the mound, he ran down the long slope in tears. He knew very well why she hadn't come for them. Her face had given it all away. How many times had she climbed to the clearing and cried for help? And then back down to her brother to try to get him to his feet. David could feel her screaming 'I wanted to!' He had just explained it to his mother on the way there, yet he had still gotten mad. Calling her stupid burned in his belly like hot coals. Why would he do such a thing?

Did he know even now? He glanced away from the stretching slope of highway, past the guard rails of the bridge they were crossing, to the thick shrubbery hiding the Pearl River. This was the second time they had crossed it. Like most of the waterways in Mississippi it probably doubled back on itself. The first time the water had been wide and deeply muddy. Here was only the barest of creeks hidden beneath the summer growth. He had no idea why he continued to think about her, why he wanted to relive the pain. He wasn't much of a fighter. His frustration and shame always got in the way. And he would hurt her – whom he loved.

That part of it could be said easily enough, the 'I love...' – it was the rest of it that was impossible: the events that shine close to the eye as cameos captured in raindrops on a leaf, events that dissolved when touched and could never be expressed. His solution had been to look for the understanding already in their faces. How could he tell his father the truth? Blurting it out might have helped a sore conscience, but it wouldn't help her. The simple facts would have only made him outraged.

He could almost see his father's face, the night before their fight, in the dim light from the lamp on the end table. The message in his expression was clear. He was poised on the couch next to the indentation of crushed springs he had created by relaxing there night after night. His head was bowed, exposing the graying hair in his part. Gnarled and hairy forearms rested limply on his thighs and his fingers were intertwined for the moment. As he began to talk, the hands would separate and he would absently pick at his fingernails.

"Son," he said, and then paused, as if the word imparted his responsibility of regret. That dismissed, he could proceed with the task at hand. His mouth seemed to be sucking on a grain of sand, preparing and polishing the sounds before they were spoken.

"I think it's high time you stopped spending so much time with Caroline."

"Why?"

"You're getting old enough to start looking around for a girlfriend. You won't find one next door."

"I don't want to see anybody else."

David didn't want to hear the reasons behind his father's request. The truth of the matter held him hot with shame and left him frightened of what might come out if he argued. His father wasn't going to understand. Beyond the open kitchen door, his mother was moving among the dishes and refrigerator, her slippered feet padding about on the tile floor made bright by fluorescent light. Her sounds were reassuring, as if nothing had changed or would change. She must not have known he was going to bring this up with David. She hadn't noticed their seriousness yet.

"I know how you feel," his father said. "But you give yourself some time and you'll feel different. You've been a good boy. Your mother has indulged you a mite too much now and then, but you've always minded us. Haven't given us one problem worth speaking about."

"You don't understand!"

"Oh?" His father, surprised by David's emotion, looked up from his nails. This wasn't like the boy. He had always nodded his head and did what he was told even if he didn't agree. He might storm around, get angry with doors or stomp his feet across a room, but he wouldn't object out loud.

"You're wrong about her," David said.

"About what?"

"Mom knows. Ask her. Everybody thinks she's stupid because of that time her brother broke his legs."

"That's just one incident, son. There's a lot more to it."

"Ask her. She knows Caroline isn't stupid."

"Your mother agrees with me."

"Mom!" David was on his feet.

She came to the doorway.

"Tell him about Caroline."

"You listen to your father." She turned back to her dinner dishes.

"Wait a minute!"

But she didn't. And David couldn't go any further. His courage was gone. He stared, flushed and angry, at his father's arms and hands —those hands with their prevalent discipline – momentarily checked from contesting their authority. Left defenseless with his truth, he had no out. His father couldn't have known more than he had said. She had put him up to it without giving him the whole story. They had given him a shirt too small to wear and he couldn't wear it. And he had loved and respected them. Even now, on this highway in the sun, with this woman he barely knew, he returned to the fact that he had been young and capable of mistakes. He had made a big one, hadn't he? And he had expected his mother to back him up on top of it. Damn her.

He hated thinking about it. Nothing would change. And talking about it was ten times as bad! He would have been fine if Martha hadn't started in with all those questions. You'd think with the problems she had she would be ready to pretend the past hadn't happened. She had no business prying. Who the hell did she think she was? He drew a cigarette from his shirt as a distraction, but it didn't help. Did he look like somebody anxious to confess his sins? He angrily flicked the cigarette out the window.

"I don't need your fucking help! I don't need anybody's!"

He looked over when he didn't get a reply. She was asleep.

* * *

On some nights, Martha would slide away from the whispering breath of the child, easing across the wide bed that creaked with every turn, to lie curled at the edge, her arms wrapped about a pillow. She was barely balanced on the rim of something dark and deep. The soft shape held to her chest in yearning might have had a name, had the crumbling earth of her bitterness given her a safe place to pronounce it. But she had no footing here, the nebulous form of linen and feathers was scarcely a barrier against the tumbling down which she feared more than death. She couldn't remember him. Remembering, grasping after the amorphous and horrible arms would find her wishing for the fall, the oblivion. Only the child prevented her. The little girl's moist noises were the constant drumming of necessity. She had to hold on.

When she could sleep, when the fatigue of the long day lay upon her like a sodden lover, it was the rhythm of the child's breathing that carried her out of her knotted body to where all the heartbeats we have lain with say it's safe. And when she could sleep, she would dream of the rain. Rain running, twisting down the mud-tinged rivulet of the slick and grassy slope, turning now but never stopping, falling in a whirlpool rush down, down, down to the gush of water at the bottom. Rain on a windshield.

Rain so heavy that the brick wall beyond the glass is shrouded in a weave of grey thread. Rain which whispers in waves and echoes from the pavement like an endless crumpling of foil. Rain which slides down the glass in sheets of thin liquid. And she would wake cold and tense, and wet with sweat.

Chapter Eight

The little girl stirred first. The back of her head appeared in David's rearview mirror just before he started up another long hill and as the car was chugging and growing more sluggish by the minute, he ignored her. The gas pedal was nearly to the floor by the time he reached the crest. They had slowed to thirty miles an hour. When he eased off and glanced up again, she was gone. Her tiny voice was discussing something very wisely with the back seat or the blanket, but he couldn't make out what she was saying.

"You awake there?" he asked.

She stood up in the seat and nodded into the mirror. Was it the subdued look or the sleepiness in her eyes that reminded him of Caroline? He waved at her reflection and tried to think of a way to bring her into the front seat without being distracted from the road. He was gunning down the slope to gain momentum for the next hill.

"Can you stay back there until we stop or until your grandmother wakes up?"

Martha groaned loudly. He looked and found the woman cringing in the corner, her hands clawing the air before her. The car was lurching again at the start of the incline. He grabbed her shoulder and shook her.

"What? What?" Martha asked feebly.

"Lisa."

Martha sat up suddenly and turned to the back seat with a frightened glance.

"What?"

The car chugged even more violently as he forced it to the top.

"Don't ever do that again." Martha told him. She was pulling Lisa into the front seat. "You scared me half to death!"

"You were having a nightmare."

"I was? I don't remember. What's wrong with the car?"

"I don't know. The spark plugs maybe."

"Why didn't you check them before we left?"

"When did I have time to check the goddamn plugs?" he asked angrily.

"You should have taken the time!"

"We're going to have to stop," he said.

"I don't want to hear you complain about being behind schedule. This is your fault."

"We won't get anywhere at this rate," he murmured.

"That would suit you, wouldn't it?"

"Oh yeah, I'd just love being stranded out in the middle of nowhere with some old bitch."

That silenced her. When the explosion he expected didn't come, he glanced at her cautiously. A tear had streaked her cheek. He bent over the steering wheel.

"I shouldn't have said what I did," he told her.

She didn't answer.

"Hey, I'm sorry."

"I'm all right. You shouldn't have woken me up so quick, is all. I thought something was wrong with Lisa. You scared me."

"You looked like you were drowning in your dreams."

"You really think I'm that old?" she asked.

"No."

"They say women reach their prime at my age."

"We need to watch for a place to stop."

"It's too bad men are past theirs at twenty."

"You do have bad dreams. They all like that one?" he asked.

"Mostly. Ever since George died."

"I got to potty," Lisa said.

"We'll stop in just a minute, darling," she said. "I wish I could remember them. But then again maybe it's better that I don't."

"I don't recall mine either," David said. He had just spotted a gas station sign.

The car took the exit ramp as if it was the last thing it would do. By the time they reached the small two-lane highway at the top, David was hunched forward on the wheel, pushing for all he was worth. The gas pedal had been forced to the floor long ago. He eased off only momentarily before the stop sign and the engine backfired, exploding loudly. Pulling across into the cracked concrete lot of the old station, he passed the two dirty pumps sitting out front and parked beside the office. Martha peered at the building.

"Is it open?" she asked.

With a sudden movement inside, a fixture became a large pot-bellied man rising from a stool in the corner. He appeared in the open doorway and gaped back at them. David turned off the ignition and the car shuddered and died.

They climbed out, stiff-legged and awkward in their first steps. Martha helped the girl down and led her off to the back corner of the building where the restroom sign stuck out. David nodded to the attendant – the man seemed a statue – then stretched and walked through his dizziness to the trunk. Twice through the boxes didn't produce any tools so he gave up suddenly, feeling tired. He hoped if they were in the trailer they were near the door. Returning to the front of the car, he nodded once more to the fat man. Again there was no response. He sat next to the dent in the hood and looked out at the freeway and the rolling hills ahead of them. This was meadowland, a thick blanket rumpled from sleep. Except for the gray strip highway, its borders of fresh orange clay and evenly-spaced baby pines, there was little obstruction before the thick trees atop the next ridge. From the faded blue sky, a child's hand might reach down to set toy soldiers there in a gully, or a cannon there on a hillside. How lifeless it was. There weren't any birds singing or any sense of wind. Only the occasional dry sandpaper sound of a car passing on the highway reminded him that this wasn't a place to pull the covers up, to sleep like a child with a fever whose toys lay forgotten in folds of warm cloth. As he watched Lisa return hand in hand with Martha, he saw without envy the futility of his desire. His turn had come and gone long ago.

"So what's the problem with the car?" Martha asked.

"I couldn't find any tools."

"There's a big red toolbox in the trunk."

"Not in this trunk."

She released the girl's hand and went back to see for herself. David followed, keeping one eye out for Lisa. Martha rummaged through the boxes without success. She stared at him for a moment with a puzzled look as if she were trying to recall if they had been packed and put in the trailer.

"The bitch!" she said.

"What –"

"Kathy! She must have taken them! Now what will we do?"

"Maybe I can get one from the attendant." David ground out the cigarette butt under his shoe and approached the big man who hadn't moved from the doorjamb since they had arrived.

"Howdy." The man's immobile face twitched. "We're in a pinch here. I was wondering if you could loan us a wrench."

"Can't loan tools."

"I'll probably have to buy new plugs, so you'd be making money."

"You want me to replace the plugs, I can do that. Can't loan tools."

"We don't have much money. That's why I'm asking for the favor."

The man just looked at him. "You own this joint?"

"No."

"How about calling the owner for permission?"

"No."

"Have a heart. If I don't get it running, we'll have to spend the night here. The little girl is sickly anyhow. She shouldn't be sleeping in a car."

The man's eyes blinked, so David waited, hoping that he was thinking it over. When the silence stretched on, it became apparent that he wasn't going to answer at all.

"Your answer is still no?" David asked finally.

"Can't loan tools."

"How about sticking your goddamn wrench up your mother-fucking ass!" David angrily turned back to the car.

Martha was waiting for him beside the open passenger door.

"What did you say to him?" she demanded.

"Never mind. Let's get out of here."

"Hold on. I'll talk to him."

David started to blow up at her, but caught himself. She would fight back.

"Be my guest."

Off she went. He didn't want to watch. Something told him she would succeed, although he couldn't imagine how. As of yet the fat man hadn't moved from his original pose, despite all the smiles and sweetness she had turned on upon reaching him.

"David."

Lisa was standing before him with her arms outstretched. He picked her up and sat her on the front fender.

"What you got there?" he asked.

"A rock."

"Let's see."

She handed it to him. The stone was an ordinary piece of white gravel. The sunlight was making it sparkle a bit.

The fat man had turned and entered the office with Martha close on his heels. Perhaps she wasn't going to do it after all.

"That's pretty. You know how to turn it off?"

Lisa shook her head.

"Put it in your hand and put your other hand over it. Like this."

She gazed at the rock in the shadow of her hand and began to frown.

"It goes to sleep when it's dark. Move your hand and it will wake up again."

She made the rock sparkle again.

"I didn't know you knew how to smile," David said. "Who taught you that?"

She shrugged. He looked up to find Martha walking toward them with the wrench in her hand. All he could do was shake his head.

Martha slapped the tool into his hand with a smirk.

"What did you say to him?"

"Never you mind." She lifted Lisa down and helped him open the hood.

He started with the plug that looked the easiest to reach. The engine was still hot, the space crowded and the brace on his finger was too large so it was slow going. He was beginning to get irritated: he could feel Martha's impatience standing close beside him.

"Ouch! Damn it!" He sucked on a knuckle. This wasn't going to work. He tried his left hand, and despite its awkwardness, he found he could turn the wrench without getting burnt. The plug finally came free. He dropped it on the fender.

"What did I tell you," he said.

Her brow and lips grew hard and seemed about to settle into a scowl when she sucked her cheeks in suddenly, as if she were holding her breath and her anger as well.

"We've got to buy new ones," she said.

"Looks like it."

"I don't suppose you've got any money."

"No. You said you'd pay expenses."

"Well, if it was me trying to be such an expert about cars, I'd feel a mite responsible when I was wrong."

"You want me to pay you back?" David asked.

"No. That's all right." She was going after her purse in the front seat. "I just wish you had been honest to say you didn't know anything."

She handed him a two twenties.

"Will that be enough?"

"I don't know."

"A fine one you are. Get us some soda pop while you're there, would you?"

He had almost stuck the bills in his pocket when he realized his hands were greasy. Gathering up the still warm plug, he approached the attendant hesitantly. He was sure he would have to pay his dues for cussing him out a minute ago.

"I need a set of these."

"How many?" The man had accepted the spark plug easily enough.

"I don't know."

He returned to the car.

"What now?" Martha asked.

"How many cylinders you got?"

They counted them together and David went back. It was hard to keep a straight face. The man thought he was a fool — and he was probably right.

"Six."

The man stirred, accepted a bill and sauntered back into the office. After a moment, he returned with change and the packages of plugs.

"You got change for the pop machine?" David asked.

Again he disappeared without the slightest rancor. David began to wonder what Martha had told him. He was acting too calm. The man handed over the quarters and resumed his position against the doorsill.

"Nice weather today," David said.

He nodded.

"Makes you want to go jump in a lake."

The man squinted. David gave up. Buying the pop, he balanced them atop the plugs and went to the car.

"Reminds me of Baby Huey," David said as he held out his handful for her to take the cans.

She glanced at the attendant and then turned away from the station so he wouldn't see her smile.

As David went to work, Martha opened the packages and set the plugs neatly in a row on the fender. She had finished and was sipping her pop while he was still trying to get the first one in.

"Shit," he said.

The plug slipped from his hand and dropped from sight. There was a clunk somewhere. She crouched down and lowered her head below the chrome bumper. Her lace bra was exposed again.

"It's down here."

He got down and scraped the gravel with his left hand to retrieve it.

"Need some help?" she asked.

"Cup your hand underneath."

Managing to get the threads started, he grabbed the wrench only to find that tightening it was going to be a clumsy chore as well. Her warm arm against his own wasn't helping him concentrate.

"Here. I'll hold it. You turn," he told her.

"Like this?"

"You got it."

"I might be a mechanic yet if this is all there is to it," she said.

"You could go into business. Bilk tourists and little old ladies."

"Just young men."

David took over the wrench to give it one last shove and then replaced the lead wire.

"Ready to do the next one?" she asked.

They removed the second plug and she started to screw in its replacement.

"You have to take the thing off the end," he said.

"You know what?" she asked, twisting the cover off the top of the plug.

"What?"

"You need a haircut."

She brushed back a lock of hair that had fallen across his forehead. Her finger left a grease mark.

"Oops. Sorry."

"What?" He looked up at her. Her face was inches from his. Those large brown eyes were glowing happily and she seemed on the verge of something.

"Where's Lisa?" he asked.

"In the car. She got bored with us. I'm getting your pretty face all dirty."

David felt warm. He didn't know how she could say a thing like that. Then, suddenly, as if it had been discussed enough, as if they had seen into each other's thoughts and knew at last it was safe, they moved together, their lips touched and paused for a moment, and tumbled into a passionate embrace. He squeezed her to him, wanting nothing else. She was beautiful to hold. Her body stretched to his, the curve of her waist, her breasts against him – all this saying that she wanted him – magnified his desire.

He might have continued to press, to move further toward what he thought they both wanted, what they had always wanted, but with that hesitation, the slightest of withdrawals which new lovers may intuit beforehand like one may foresee the first hairline crack in a vibrant fertile egg, she paused for breath. He sighed and paused as well. They hugged once more briefly and parted, conscious of their surroundings and the task they had yet to finish. The wrench had grown awkward in his hand.

She seemed a bit chagrined too.

"Maybe I should smear some more – if this is what's going to happen." She reached for him with her greasy hands. He jerked back and retreated when she pursued him.

"Stop!"

"Chicken," she called.

He scowled at her. She acted as if she were going to cup his face in her palms, but stopped just short of actually touching him.

"I was only teasing," she said.

"We need to get the plugs changed so we can get out of here."

"All right. One more little peck for the road?"

He obliged her and they went back to work. As they bent over the engine now, she was right up against him. Her hips were next to his, her arm was tickling the hair on his arm. In reaching past him for another spark plug, her breast brushed the back of his hand. The imagined impression of soft flesh lingered, even though he wished it away. He tried not to look at her. The seriousness of what they had done was too clear: he was trapped into something he wasn't sure he wanted. There was too much wrong with her face. Too many wrinkles, too much slack skin on her neck. Her cheeks were speckled with down that was turning grey. He might be able to ignore what he saw if he worked at it, or if it were dark, but in the immediate bright afternoon he was ready to shun her touch. If only he could do it without hurting her feelings. It wasn't her fault that she was old. He hoped his aversion wouldn't show until he could figure out a good way to tell her.

"We make a pretty good team," she said. They were almost finished.

"Couldn't have done it without you."

"You'll have to change that bandage."

"I didn't bring anything." He finally looked at her.

"I'll find something."

David stood up from the engine and stretched his arms behind him to ease his stiff back. She turned and leaned against the front grill, swiping at a lock of hair that had fallen in her eyes.

"How do we get this stuff off?" she asked and then pointed at his white pants. There was a large grease smear on his leg.

"Shit!"

"How did you do that? We were being careful."

"When you were chasing me."

"I would have known it if I did, Davey."

"We'll need some gasoline."

"You want me to go ask?"

"You have better luck," he said.

He handed her the wrench. While she went about her errand, he gathered up the loose wrappers and old plugs and carried them to the trash can out by the gas pump. Behind the dusty windowpanes of the office, she was waving her arms at the fat man. She's got guts, he thought, she doesn't give up. He respected her, he didn't know why it was so hard to be fair with her. The spot on his pants wasn't her fault, but he had blamed her anyway. He'd have to apologize for that. After a moment, the attendant emerged with a bucket in his hand. Martha was close on his heels like a terrier yapping after a wayward calf. They came out to the pump. The bucket was set down with an indignant clunk. The fat man yanked the gas nozzle free and began to fill it.

"Good thing you bought them plugs," he said.

"Yeah?" David asked.

"That's all I got to say."

The bucket was lifted out away from the pump and a rag was disdainfully offered from his coveralls' hip pocket. Martha took it and he stomped away.

"Come here," she told David.

He stepped up and let her rub at the spot on his leg. The grease seemed to be coming off, but she was getting it so soaked that it was hard to tell. The skin under the cloth tingled and then began to burn.

"That's plenty," he said. Kneeling beside her, he washed his hands in the bucket. "Hey. What did you tell that fat guy about me?"

"That you had just got home from Vietnam and you were still pretty crazy." She smiled mischievously.

"You're such a liar."

She tossed the rag to him and stood up.

"I'm going to wash with soap and water. This stinks to high heaven."

When he finished he carried the gasoline to the edge of the concrete to dump it. Grease strands floated out across the rocks and sank limply as the pool was absorbed by the dry ground. He raked the gravel with his foot. On his way to return the bucket, he suddenly remembered that Lisa was alone in the car. As soon as he changed direction, the fat man was back outside, striding after him.

"Hey! You!"

David turned.

"The bucket!"

David waited for him to get close and feigned throwing it at him. His arms jerked up in self-protection. David tried to leer at him. The fat man approached more cautiously and although it was handed over to him calmly, he seemed skittish.

"Mighty valuable thing to have," David said. The man wasn't going to answer. "You know what we did with buckets in 'Nam?"

"What?"

David wanted to say something nasty or make up something crazy to scare him, but he got embarrassed by what he was doing.

"Damned if I know."

The man cocked his head. David walked away from him quickly.

Martha had already returned to the car. Lisa was inside, leaning against the steering wheel, trading funny faces with her through the windshield, so David went to wash his hands. When he returned, Martha was waiting with a clean strip of cloth for his finger. The fabric was a faded print with tiny flowers, the same print dress she had worn that morning.

"Where did this come from?" he asked.

"Never you mind."

She snipped off the wet bandage with a pair of cuticle scissors and dried the finger with a paper napkin.

"I thought you cut it."

"Just smashed it." He held up the other hand for comparison.

Replacing the brace, she wrapped the lavender strip around it securely and brought up the ends.

"Shall I tie it in a bow?"

"I have to drive with it."

"There." She looked down at his pants and touched the spot. It was dry. Some of the grease remained and the gasoline had left a larger yellow halo.

"You got another pair of pants?"

"No."

"Next time I'll get the other leg as well so at least you'll match."

"There'd better not be a next time."

"So do I get a thank you?" she asked.

They were both self-conscious. He bent down to kiss her carefully and gently, as if for the first time. From the corner of his eye, he noticed Lisa watching them intently.

Chapter Nine

Gravel scrunching under tires is almost the sound of home. Watching dusk, when the sky is red and storm clouds are embroidered orange, can be akin to watching those whitewashed porch slats turn the color of steel in the fading light. And when the air is cool, you can almost taste the run up the grass to take a turn on the handle of the ice cream maker as much as you can taste the ice cream itself. With evening this nostalgia may seep into your pores as a familiar companion to the growing darkness, and the strangest settings may become a place to arrive. He had found such a shelter in the keep of the black trailer trucks. Beyond a gap, the yellow diner glared. The sky above burned wildly and the heavy-handed clouds reaching for the sunset would make it dark soon. Drops of rain could be felt but not seen. Brush piles, strung along the opposite side of the highway, were smoldering and collapsing into heaps of glowing ember. The road crew's voices were incantations to the deepening shadows in the pines. And he knew that if this was home, it was home at the end of the highway, at the end of the world, where the top of the next hill would crumble off into starless sea.

There was nothing to do but pretend that their journey would continue. He imagined picking Lisa up in his arms, and with Martha wobbling alongside in her heels, they would cross the gravel toward the yellow windows. The wind would send wisps of the girl's hair across his lips.

The little girl was asleep in the back seat. He looked at Martha and they reached for each other. Her tongue was in his mouth. His fingers unbuttoned her blouse. He could ignore her wrinkles. This was caring, respectful, gentle. She brought his hand between her legs. He was smothered, he was hard, he was lost.

Lisa woke up.

"Where?" she asked.

They separated and stared out of the front windshield, trying to breathe calmly.

As they walked out of the black trailers, a truck's engine roared and one side rolled away with its cab to expose the diner's wide interior, the row upon row of red booths and salmon-colored tabletops. Amidst the disarray of plates and speckled chrome, sallow-faced men ate, picked their teeth, or laughed at one another. A smoke cloud hung, suspended, just above their heads. Tightly-waisted women served them.

"You'll protect us?" Martha asked at his shoulder.

David glanced at her dubiously.

When they entered, every face turned to look. They paused at the glass case and cash register, momentarily dumbfounded by the clash of garish colors. The shallow green highway ached in their eyes like dust. Dishes clattered about them. There was no one to show them the way and the cashier seemed suddenly occupied. So David, crossing the room self-consciously, brought them to an empty booth. One by one, the faces returned to eating or talking. The ease with which they were being ignored was heartening until Martha tried to get the attention of a waitress. None of the women seemed to want to come near them.

As Lisa was still standing up in the booth for the lack of a booster seat, David got up again to find one. Two waitresses were standing idle beside some toasters. They looked away when he approached them. One took a fingernail file from her apron and began to file her nails.

"Excuse me."

They both glanced up a bit startled. Their noses twitched as if they were trapped rabbits.

"Do you have a child's seat?"

The one with the fingernail file shook her head slowly.

"You have anything for the little girl to sit on?"

"I'll... I'll find you something."

"Can we get waited on?"

"Have a seat, sir."

David turned as they edged away from him. He returned to the booth embarrassed and angry and wouldn't sit down.

"Let's get out of here."

"Cool off. Aren't you hungry?" Martha asked.

"I don't even know if we're going to get waited on here."

"Sit down and we'll see. A few minutes won't hurt."

He sat.

A waitress appeared after a moment, bearing a booster seat. She was an older woman with hair that stood stiffly in ringlets atop her head. Her face cracked open into a big smile and it looked as though a piece of cheek or a fragment of chin might fall and shatter like porcelain on the floor.

"Hello!" She was addressing Lisa. "Those girls don't know much, do they?"

Once the little girl was situated, she ran off and returned with water and menus.

"And what's your name?" She hadn't looked at Martha and David yet.

Lisa shook her head.

"Are you hungry? You don't talk much, do you?"

"She's shy around strangers," Martha told her.

"Grandma says you're shy. You don't look shy to me."

And she was off again across the restaurant.

Martha suddenly began digging in her purse and pulled out her wallet to count her money below the table edge.

"I haven't got enough for all of us to eat."

"How much do you have?" David had a five-dollar bill, but he didn't want to spend it. It was to keep him in cigarettes.

"Enough for two. Why don't you eat with Lisa?"

"What about you?"

"I had chicken earlier. You haven't eaten all day."

"We can split something," David said.

Martha patted his hand and held it.

"I'm not hungry," she said. "You're nice when you want to be."

"How are we supposed to get to Nashville if you're out of money?"

"I can write a check when we get to my brother's farm. He always has cash around. Doesn't believe in –"

The waitress had returned. She stared at their hands together in the middle of the table. David withdrew his cautiously.

"I hope I didn't offend you by calling you Grandma," she told Martha.

"Oh, I'm Grandma all right."

"You ready?"

They ordered.

"Where's your restroom?" Martha asked.

"Over there."

When Martha got up and bent over to help Lisa out, her cleavage opened before them like a blossom. The waitress pointed it out to him with her eyes and smirked.

"She's paying me to take her to Nashville," he blurted.

Martha looked up surprised. There was a brief moment of awkward silence and then the hurt began to melt into her face.

"He comes cheap," she said. Grabbing Lisa's hand, she marched off to the restroom.

David was ready for the red vinyl seat to fold up and swallow him. He turned to the waitress only to find that she had gone away as well. Being left alone made it worse. Why had he opened his mouth at all? Who cared what some old biddy thought! He stared off across the restaurant, unable to think of anything he could say to her when she returned. The serving window from the kitchen was directly in front of him. The movement of the white shirts beyond the stainless steel didn't register with him until, suddenly, he recognized their order sitting in the window under the heat lamp's orange glow. It had been there for some time. Was the woman waiting for Martha to come back? She was taking an awful long time. He looked around but didn't see the waitress. Perhaps she had gone to talk to Martha. That was a silly idea. She might have shown Martha how to leave by the back door. Jumping up, he rushed to the first empty space along the outside window and pressed his face against the black glass. The car and trailer were still there, a deserted silhouette punctuated by the smoldering fires across the highway. As he returned to the table, Martha appeared at the other end of the dining room. The waitress came out of the same hallway right after her. David would pretend he hadn't noticed. He was in enough trouble.

He apologized when she reached the table.

"No," she replied, helping Lisa up. "I've decided you're right. You're driving us to Nashville out of kindness. I've got no reason to suppose it's anything more."

"I've been thinking about your offer of having me stay there with you."

"I don't want to talk about it right now. I just got my feelings hurt. I guess I was beginning to fall in love with you. And I thought you were feeling the same way."

The waitress brought their food. She totaled the check, laid it on the table, and rolled her eyes skyward for his benefit. He looked after her in amazement.

"What did you say to her?" he asked.

"Who?"

Martha didn't seem to be playing dumb. He waved his hand in dismissal.

"What are you going to do there with a car and no license?"

"We did just fine before you showed up."

"That's not what you were saying earlier," he said.

"I don't remember what I said. Whatever it was, I didn't mean it. That's what you always say, isn't it?"

David couldn't reply.

"Sit up straight, young lady." Lisa was sliding off her booster seat. Taking the girl's plate, Martha cut up the hamburger and added a dollop of ketchup next to the French fries. Lisa ate a few of the fries, but then began to play with the food: pushing pieces of hamburger into the mound of ketchup and leaving them there. "Stop playing and eat." She speared a piece of hamburger with her fork and popped it into the little girl's mouth.

"I could at least give you driving lessons," David said.

"I can drive just fine, thank you. I'm paying for that food, so you'd better not let it go to waste."

He hadn't touched his own plate.

"You want to cut it up for me?"

"Aren't you smart?"

"I'm smart enough to know how to drive a car," he said.

"Give me the keys."

"What for?"

"It's my car," she said. "Give me the keys!"

He didn't want to, but he dug in his pocket and produced them.

"I'm driving as far as my brother's tonight. You can either come along for the ride or you can stay here."

"How am I supposed to get back to New Orleans if I stay?"

"The deal was a bus ticket for getting us to Nashville. Not one third of the way. What's it going to be?"

"I guess I'm riding with you."

"Good. We'll see if you're smart enough to ride in a car as well."

She waved the waitress over and asked for a doggie bag and the check.

"You're going bye-bye?" the woman asked Lisa.

"We're in a hurry," Martha replied.

"No need to get your dander up."

She carried their plates away.

"I don't know if you want to stay at my brother's and find your own way back to New Orleans or go on with me, but I'm going to make it a quick stop. I'm only going to be there long enough to pick up some of my things and then go on."

"You don't want to sleep?" David asked.

"No."

"Why?"

"Lisa's mother may be there. I don't want any more problems than I've got. You understand?"

"I understand I've got to eat on the run and go without sleep."

"You decide what you want," she said.

The waitress had returned with the bag. Martha accepted the check, studied it and grabbed her purse.

"You can carry Lisa out to the car," she said and got up to go to the cashier.

David, angry at being ordered around, stared after her for a moment and then stood up perplexed. She hadn't given him a choice. He couldn't leave the little girl here by herself. Hoisting her out of the seat, he started for the door. Martha was leaving ahead of them. Fuck her, he thought.

"I brought your dinner with us," he told Lisa, holding up the bag.

She reached for it. He was opening the bag as he backed through the glass door, but stopped when he saw the weather outside. Rain was falling heavily. The bonfires across the road were reduced to streaming clouds of white smoke. Martha was already running for the car.

"We'd better wait till we're out of this," he said.

And he ran too. Across the large and slippery gravel, while trying to protect her head, knowing she would get wet anyway, and wondering how Martha had managed it in her high heels. They were soaked by the time he had the car door open. Lisa began sniveling once they were safe inside. Martha pulled the blanket out of the back seat to dry her off.

"You should have waited by the door! I would've brought the car over!" she said angrily.

"I didn't think that would occur to you."

"If she gets sick it'll be your fault!"

David took the fries from the soggy bag and held one out to Lisa. She accepted it tentatively and then reached for the rest to hold in her lap against her sorrow.

"You happy?" David asked Martha.

She finished wrapping Lisa in the blanket and fumbled with the ignition. Her hands were shaking. The car started, but then she seemed at a loss.

"The lights are there," David said. "Why don't you pull the seat up?"

His knees were soon against the dash. She put the car in drive and bent over the wheel to peer out the wet windshield.

"The wipers."

"All right! How do we get out of here?"

"There's a turnaround past the building."

She drove on.

"Can you see it?" she asked.

"You just passed it. You'll have to back up."

She braked and put it in reverse. In twisting to get a better view in the side mirror, she turned the steering wheel in the same direction without thinking.

"Don't turn anymore!" David said.

The trailer was already turning out into the mud.

"Stop!"

The car jerked to a halt.

"Don't you shout at me!"

"Can you see at night?" he asked.

"Of course I can see."

"The turnout is in front of you."

"I know that!"

She carefully put the car back into drive and gripped the wheel. In the light from the dash her knuckles looked stiff and bloodless. She wasn't breathing.

"Relax," David said. "It's a left turn."

She managed to stay on the gravel, even though David knew she had guessed at where the road forked. They came around by the front of the diner again. The yellow windows and motionless interior seemed a grainy photograph behind the haze of rain. A flash of lightning made the building whole for a split second, and then it was gone. They moved away coldly. The car and trailer bounced onto the little highway that led to the freeway ramp. At the top, Martha slowed and almost stopped to look before pulling out.

As she seemed to be taking a long time to gain speed, David leaned toward the speedometer for a look. She was holding the car just above forty.

"You can go a little faster," he said.

"You're the race car driver, I'm not. The speed limit is fifty-five."

"You're not even doing that. A truck coming up behind you going ninety won't be able to brake fast enough to avoid hitting you."

"He shouldn't be going ninety."

"It won't matter what he should or shouldn't be doing."

After a moment, she stepped on the gas and brought the needle up to sit between fifty-five and sixty.

David knew he would have to be happy with that. Flicking the defroster on, he stretched and drew Lisa on to his lap. The container of French fries soon joined the crumpled bag at his feet and she nestled, grasping the brace on his finger as she sucked her thumb. The highway ahead was a low tunnel of black pavement and rain. With each flash of lightning the forest jumped, wavering like smoke, in the fogged side window. If there was thunder, it was hidden in the endless drone of engine and fan. Against the now closed night, he found himself looking at his own face, and for a moment it was the empty shell of someone else, etched nearly lifeless in the glass. He was the ghost. Tenuous except for the weight of the little girl. And was that anything more than just his resemblance to her father, a yearning for an impression of lap and shirt buttons? He struggled to regain the feel of his skin. She was a memory as well, another little girl in another place. Perhaps that was all that could be expected: the communion of cobwebs, orphans in a box riding nowhere.

He must have dozed, for when he was suddenly thrown against the door he was confused. Their tires were rattling over the gravel of the shoulder. Martha was fighting the wheel. The huge black slab of a truck shot past them in the other lane, its taillights gleaming. He grabbed and held the steering wheel against her attempt to swing it strongly back to the pavement.

"Ease it back on," he shouted. "You're all right."

He let go once they were on the highway again.

"I'm sick of your yelling."

"You tired of driving yet?"

"No. Go back to sleep."

"I'm supposed to sleep through this?" He rubbed his eyes and reached for a cigarette. Lisa was getting resettled in his lap.

"That stinks," Martha said.

He opened the side vent.

The night gushed in. The quick coolness and the tiny spatter of deflected rain sent a chill through his shoulders. They came to the top of another hill and below, ahead of them, a swarm of red taillights sat like frozen fireflies in the murk. They were gaining on them. For an instant, they seemed not to be moving at all. Then with a slight rocking of black against black, they became the huge shadows of trucks, forms without silhouettes. They were moving cautiously, lined up now in the slow lane despite the other lane being clear. Martha barreled down on the last one, bringing the car up to within feet of the giant mud flaps before hitting the brakes. David was pushing a hole through the floor with his foot. She slowed until the truck's draft hit them and began to rock the trailer.

"How fast are you going?"

She didn't answer. She fought the wheel for a moment and then swerved to the outside lane to pass. The draft made her weave from side to side as she drew abreast of the churning tires. David gripped the armrest as they reached the cab. Lisa woke up.

"You shouldn't pass him! There's probably a speed trap!"

The semi slowed dramatically to let her pass. Ahead were two more cars and another truck, all sitting in the right lane. He expected her to pull in behind the first car but she kept right on going.

Passing the cars was easily done. But as she neared the next truck she began to sway back and forth again. David didn't know what to do. Her face was gray and frozen. Her arms were trembling. Grabbing the wheel might startle her

133

and cause the accident he was trying to avoid. He was afraid to look at the speedometer.

"I can't do this!" she suddenly cried.

"Pretend it isn't there!"

He helped her steady the wheel. Lisa had wrapped her arms around his other arm.

The second truck slowed before they reached its taillights. They shot by.

There was a car ahead in their lane. She reduced her speed as she approached and when she was about fifty feet away she hit the gas again.

"What are you doing?" David asked desperately.

They were ten feet from the car. Then five. Finally she braked.

"That damn truck is on my tail!"

"Pull over."

"I can't."

David turned to see what was behind them in the slow lane, but the windows were fogged. Rolling his down, he hugged Lisa to his chest and stuck his head out. She whimpered. The nearest car was a hundred yards back.

"You've got room. Change lanes."

She lurched to the right with the trailer swinging wildly behind them. There was an exit immediately ahead. She rushed up the ramp without the slightest hesitation.

"Slow down!"

The tires skidded over the pavement. At the top of the overpass, she pulled off to the shoulder and stopped abruptly. She slammed the stick into Park and jumped from the car. Running out into the thin drizzle exposed by the headlights, she stumbled twice and then finally fell to her knees in the gravel.

"Christ," David murmured. He slid Lisa off his lap, told her to stay put and climbed out to go after her. He went slowly, conscious of his own footsteps in the gravel. His hair was plastered to his forehead by the time he reached her. Pausing a few feet away, he waited, hoping that she might notice him and return suddenly to the living, but he wasn't expecting it. This was more like waiting to see what an injured animal was going to do.

"Are you all right?"

She looked up, shielding her eyes from the glare of the lights.

"It's me. David," he said.

She was confused. She had been crying, was still crying. She was frightened. He stepped over to her and offered his hand.

"It's all right."

He helped her up and she fell into his arms, burying her face against his chest.

"I thought..." she sobbed.

"I'm David," he repeated softly. She was scaring him all over again.

She nodded into his shirt.

Beyond their headlights, the unblinking fireflies of the traffic marked the otherwise black highway. Their retreat and quick disappearance made the pit of night bottomless.

"Come on. We can't stay here," he whispered.

Chapter Ten

It was as if nothing had happened. He got her to the car, took the wheel and drove them down to the wet and empty highway. She was quiet for a long time, seeking in stillness the healing others would find in calm sleep. David didn't intrude. Silence was what he knew best. And he didn't want to look any closer at what he had glimpsed back there. When the road faded to gray again and the wipers could be shut off, her breathing seemed to grow regular.

"Are you asleep?" he asked.

"No."

"How far before I turn off for your brother's?"

"It shouldn't be long." She sounded gentle and distant. "There's an exit for Winona. Highway 82. Then you go north on 51 a little way past Duck Hill."

And she napped with his promise that he would wake her if he got confused or lost.

* * *

Within these walls, where sleep was held breathless beneath the black demon of humidity, Martha would turn and then turn again. And wake, helplessly tangled and caught in the clinging sheet. Frail legs might kick and be free but for swollen joints and sodden muscles. So she would rest here, an exhausted swimmer borne on the safety of consciousness, a damp body on the strand. She might open her eyes on the room that has been strangely silent for some time and gaze beyond the whispering form of the child. Lines of light would glow from windows shuttered in fear. A hiss would rise and fall with each passing car. And the night would not move. Softly and quietly, from that pleading part of a ruptured soul, she began a litany, an unuttered chant, a prayer for the rain that would dissolve the weight from her bed and ease the air's sad sorrow. But there will be a car and wind from the highway when the dawn finally comes. Had she forgotten? Holding that gift of vision close, she could close her eyes and pretend to sleep once more. From somewhere in the building, a leaky faucet tapped and tapped and tapped slowly, measuring out the passing seconds.

Drops of water from a gutter, falling, tumbling down walls of wet red brick, might tap the blacktop with the same sound. The lengthy silence between taps could grow longer and longer still, gutters may empty or droplets may melt into the surface of shallow puddles, until the wind moves and they fall again all at once as a memory of rain. A hand reaches for and wipes the film from the curved glass, exposing the rivulets of water and the slick alley beyond. Steam rises from the car's hood. There is a light there, beneath a tin cover, above the doorway. The doorway embedded in brick, with a railing and concrete steps down to the pavement. And the drizzle will return, murmuring now over metal and windshield, then moving, draping itself gently across the oily distance to the bottom of the railing.

And the door above will open. Heavy shoes, already growing darkly stained from the rain, will break the slick surface of the first step and pause. The cuffs of his jeans are wet. Spots appear on the shoulders of his leather jacket. He is laughing. He comes down to her. Alone, young and strong, he turns up the collar of his own jacket. Had she been invited, she would have turned it up for him. The umbrella she had brought sat half-spread on the seat beside her, droplets still clinging to the plastic. Toni appears in the doorway with her own umbrella for him. He would always be handsome, young and soaked strands of hair would lie across a forehead still wrinkled in amusement. And wiping the water from his face would reveal the awful mottled skin of her hand. If he looked at her once more with the look of a disgruntled child, she would die.

The stick shift moves under her moist fingers. Cold feet work the pedals, drawing the clutch close to breaking, gunning the engine. He will step down to the dark pavement, step down to the vibrating greens and violets of the shallow puddles, and step down into the gentle caressing curtain of rain. And tires will scream.

* * *

He found the exit easily and followed the highway markers to the little two-lane road that curved and rolled north. The sky opened here above the fields and trees, the half-moon and the legs of constellations swung up beyond each hilltop he climbed and then slid like oilcloth to lie in folds behind the leaves and fences of the bottomland. Closed and quiet porches and glaring barns were the only watchful faces in the sleeping night. The town he was to find came quickly. A grocery store, lit from deep inside, with dark gas pumps before it, a small brick post office, and houses and a white church and stoplights all turned to blinking yellow, and he was soon to the other side. He touched Martha's shoulder.

"We've gone through Duck Hill," he said.

"It's just another mile or so. There's a barn and a produce stand at the corner where we need to turn."

"You think they'll be up?"

"Probably. Did I sleep long?" she asked.

"Not very."

"I don't feel bad at all."

"It's the quiet," he said.

He took it slow, holding on to the ride. The produce stand, a gray frame leaning toward the side road, appeared and he turned into the dark tunnel of trees and gravel. He was suddenly chilled. Something would happen down here. Another turn came, this time onto dirt. He was inching forward now, avoiding the potholes he could and dipping carefully through the ones he couldn't. No scraping yet, despite the lack of room to maneuver. The drive was bordered on the left by barbed wire and on the right by a ravine that threatened his tires. They managed a curve and found the house trailer before them, lying on its side, nearly upside down below the soft shoulder. The underbelly was brightened by the moon.

"My God!" Martha gasped.

"What?"

"My trailer! Stop the car."

He braked. The ride was over.

She jumped out as if she was determined to save the trailer from its fate. Pacing off the length in measured stride, she peered down into the darkness at the other end. If there was anything to be seen, it probably made matters worse, for she returned slowly, a hand at her forehead to hold the hair from her eyes and her head shaking back and forth in disbelief. She stopped at the end exposed by his headlights and removed her shoes. The loose dirt slipped away before her feet as she tried to climb down to the window. The glass was too high. Tiptoes brought her level with the bottom sill. She looked around for something to stand on, found nothing, and clumsily made her way back up to the car. She was close to tears when she got in.

"I thought your trailer was in Nashville," David said.

"It is. This was the one I bought when I lived here. The goddamn son-of-a-bitch!"

"What?"

"I trusted him to look after it."

Her face twisted into a miserable grimace.

"They won't be happy till they take everything."

"Maybe it's not damaged that much," he said weakly.

"I hate them all!"

David touched her shoulder.

"We don't have to stop. We can just go on to Nashville," he said.

"He's not getting off that easy."

David remembered that she had to get cash here.

"Your brother has probably made plans to get it pulled out and repaired."

"You don't know how long it's been sitting here. I'm going to kill him! I just talked to him last week. Not a word. Let's go."

David drove on by the trailer and came to a gateless rickety fence. Beyond was a large yard overgrown with weeds and a two-story farmhouse. A porch light gleamed faintly. The bare bulb was swarming with moths and mosquitoes, their cloudy shadows wavering over the cracked wood and tilted pillars. The front screen sat ajar, with a gap between its top hinge and the door sill. If it hadn't been for the light, he wouldn't have thought anyone lived here. He pulled in next to a dark pickup and shut off the engine. The front door was open by the time he and Martha had climbed out. An old man, stoop-shouldered and potbellied, crossed to the front step, smoothed back his thinning hair and pulled up the strap of his overalls that had fallen from a bare shoulder. He waved to them.

Martha headed across the uneven ground toward him. David waited. Lisa was still asleep in the back seat and he was sure that there would be a fight. The cool air struck him as somehow odd and then he realized it was the stillness. The only night sounds were the locusts pulsating in unison some distance behind the house. The buzzing returned in cautious patches closer and then grew, surrounding him and drowning out the earlier chorus. This wasn't helping. He wanted to yell into the weeds, but

Martha and her brother would think he was nuts. The old man had his arms out to greet her with a hug. She swiped at his hand and he pulled in.

"I'm going to take care of that damn trailer. So you can just cool your heels," he said.

"You'd better. What I want to know is why you didn't say anything. When were you planning on telling me? You knew I was coming!"

"I was hoping to have it pulled out of there before now. This ain't my fault and I want you to stop making it out to be. We had real bad flooding this spring and that ground above the creek has never had anything to hold it together. You were the one that said where to set it."

"Why didn't you move it before it happened?"

"Some of us ain't rich."

"You just don't give a hoot about me and mine."

"Don't you talk that way to me, Missy."

Martha turned, throwing up her arms in exasperation. She looked to David, but he wasn't sure what she wanted from him so he didn't respond.

"Kathy's here," the old man said.

Martha gave up and glanced back at her brother.

"Well, I only need to get some things from the trailer and write you a check for some cash. Then we'll go."

"You can at least come in for a bite to eat."

"No time," she said. "The boy's got to be back in New Orleans by Monday morning."

"You think you can just run in and out without letting Kathy see her little one?"

"She's been drinking?"

"That don't matter!"

"Speak of the devil," Martha said.

A woman had come out on the porch. She was barefoot and sloppy in jeans rolled to mid-calf and a flannel shirt tied at the waist. Her limp blonde hair, although combed behind her ears, seemed determined to fall in her face. Her hand was soon at her cheek running back another strand.

"Hello, Mama."

The porch light cast weary shadows across her features, making her look either half-awake or half-drunk. David couldn't decide which.

"You're not looking so good," Martha said. "You've been sick?"

"You're real glowing yourself."

"Lisa's asleep. She's tired from all this traveling," Martha said.

"I bought her a present."

"I can give it to her when she wakes up tomorrow."

"I haven't been drinking. I want to see her."

"I could stop you if I've a mind too."

The daughter stepped out and touched the old man's shoulder. He ran a hand back over the top of his head.

"Come on in and have some coffee, Missy," he said. "Invite the boy too."

The daughter was already crossing to the car.

"In a minute," Martha said, following her. "I don't want Lisa to wake up frightened."

The daughter came within fifteen feet of the car and David and stopped abruptly. He was lighting a cigarette, the sudden flare of the match in his cupped hand illuminated his nose and high forehead with a sticky yellow and then an orange glow. He didn't notice her until he waved the flame out. Her face was hidden by the porch light behind her, but he could feel her eyes. What was she looking at? He must have cocked his head.

"George?"

She stepped toward him.

"George? I thought –"

"My name is David."

"What?"

"David Jacks."

"You're a ghost."

"No."

Martha, with her head bent watching the tangle of weeds and rocks, came up behind her. The daughter, startled, looked over her shoulder to see who was there. She turned on her mother.

"No!" she screamed. "This is your doing."

"What are you talking –" Martha started.

"Damn you to hell!"

She lunged for Martha, grabbed her shoulders and began shaking her.

"Haven't you punished me enough!" she screamed.

They fell, the daughter on top. She was beating Martha's head against the ground. The old man came running.

David started for them as well, unsure of what he would do when he reached them. This was unbelievable. Women didn't fight. Lisa suddenly cried out behind him. He turned. She was standing in the back seat, screaming and beating the window with her small fists. Returning to free her, he took her up in his arms and tried to comfort her, but she struggled against him, her arms flailing out to the two women. He pushed her face to his neck and swung around so that she couldn't watch. She calmed down a little. By the time he looked back, the old man had already pulled the daughter off and was helping Martha to her feet.

"Are you all right?" the old man asked.

"I think so."

She shooed his hands away and rubbed her neck. Bending her head back and then from side to side made her grimace.

"I could have gotten a concussion!" she said loudly.

The daughter, shaken by what she had done, was sitting on a rock in the high grass. Her face was hidden in her hands and limp hair.

"Come on," the old man said. "Let's go in."

"You caught me by surprise that time!" Martha shouted. "Next time I'll be ready. I'll knock your fucking block off!"

"That's enough, Missy. She's sorry. And you're shook up. Let's go in the house and sit down."

"Where's Lisa?"

Martha marched over to collect her. The little girl had stopped crying, but she was hugging David tightly, hiding in his arms, with a thumb stuck deeply in her mouth. When Martha reached for her, she recoiled against his chest.

"It's all right," David murmured. "The fighting's over."

She relaxed. Martha hefted her up and followed her brother toward the house. Lisa's face was hidden in shadow, but by the way her head was cocked over her grandmother's shoulder, he was sure she was looking back at him. He gave a small, half-hearted wave.

They entered the house. He thought of following them in, but felt he wouldn't be welcome now. He had trespassed too far and had seen too much. They couldn't be comfortable with that. Martha's daughter, still sitting with her face in her hands, was a sentinel of pain for a painful house. He wasn't to pass. He didn't understand. He wasn't sure he should. And despite what he might wish, she wasn't going to look up. What he did realize was that his presence had been the spark, the disappointment which had rekindled their grief and anger. Clearly he was not what they had hoped for. He was an interloper, a joke. A boy who thought he might fill a man's shoes. He didn't belong here.

Or anywhere. Closing the car door, he walked around to the hood and sat down to light another cigarette, feeling at odds with what he was doing. Should he even wait? He couldn't muster the impatience he would need to get them back on the road. And rushing the return to New Orleans seemed an empty gesture. He should have known better.

144

Who would want to stay in Nashville anyway? The one place he had believed in – the barn loft with the sunlight, bits of yellow straw on the wood – he couldn't bear to think of any longer. Did they think they could hurt him with this? The answer, a clear and quiet yes, he would have ripped from his heart if he could. What was he waiting for?

"You probably think I'm crazy."

Martha's daughter was standing before him, directly in front of the porch light. Shining strands of her blonde hair floated in the slight breeze, framing the silhouette of her head. Her face was a dark hole. Thrusting her hands deeper into the pockets of her jeans, she shifted her weight to expose the bare bulb behind her. David squinted and raised a hand to his forehead.

"I don't think I understand what's going on," he said.

"It wasn't fair to put you through that."

David shrugged.

"I couldn't help but notice how Lisa clung to you. You must be treating her real nice for her to take to you that way. She needs a lot of loving and I wanted to thank you for whatever you're doing for her."

"I like her."

"We've had rough time." Her voice cracked. "I'm not much good for anything. It's not that I don't love her, you see, it's just..."

David couldn't see her crumpled face or the tears, but he could sense them in her voice.

"And there's nobody to help anymore." She leaned on the other foot, blocking the porch light again. "You look like George. I don't sleep well. Seems like I'm tired all the time. Sometimes if I only close my eyes, I see him – so close I could almost reach out and touch him. I don't know when I'm dreaming and when I'm awake."

"You're Kathy."

"Mama mentioned me?"

She turned as if to go before he could reply. Her face in the light looked wooden and colorless. She paused, absently, and seemed to be talking to the driveway rather than to him.

"You must be tired from driving all night. I'm not being hospitable. Let me go make peace with my mother so you can come in and have something to eat or something."

She walked to the house. David watched her go in, watched the screen door lean back awkwardly and then swing after her, scraping along the porch floor on its one remaining hinge. The insects were resuming their dance about the bulb. A few of the larger moths were disappearing and reappearing from the gap between door and sill. No one seemed to care. David wanted to go push it shut. Make it perfect. Squeeze out the dust of the moths. Squeeze in all the rust-colored faces that dared to look out.

His own mother's face grew rust-colored in shadows. Was it fair to hate his mother now? He had been aware of her in some other room when he came back to their house after the fight with his father and brother. He hadn't wanted to see her. He had moved through the house as if any undue emotion or noise might erase her, leaving the house empty and barren. He had gone to the kitchen and held his bloody palm under the cold and slight stream from the tap. Too much water would make the pipes moan. And he wrapped the wound in a dishcloth, pulling the knot tight with his teeth. Then down the hall to his bedroom to throw some clothes in a knapsack. He gained the front screen freely and hesitated there, the cry almost forcing itself from his lips before he could stop it. There was nowhere to go but out. He made the door silent and complete. And he would have escaped unscathed, leaving the world there behind him intact and untouched, if he hadn't turned at the gate to look back. His mother was standing behind the dark screen. She was frozen and blurred like an underdeveloped photograph. He waited, searching the eyes he couldn't see, but could imagine. She was about to call after him, wasn't she? And as he waited, it came to him that she would never call out to him. He would stand there until the sun fell and the night grew cold around him and she would turn and disappear when some duty called, disappear back into the small routines that inhabited the house like so many dead children and she would never hear from him what happened or why he had left or why his hand was bleeding. And nothing would change that now. He turned from the bulb and crooked screen, suddenly unwilling to bear the brunt of the light and the house beyond where these people lived. The moths would come and go as they pleased. He couldn't watch.

He found a ragged path in the high weeds beside the house and stumbled upon stepping into the darkness there. Passing below the orange windows, he descended to where a creek opened before him like a silver frown. The locusts were softer here. The water gurgled, spun, bubbled and gushed with energy. There was moonlight and the sudden coolness of the night air made him shiver. He cupped his hands, breaking them to scrub his face. The cold made him shiver. His finger ached. God, was he tired. His fatigue had been hiding, waiting for him here. Now the urge to make a small nest in the weeds, to crawl in and curl up next to the water, seemed the only thing left to do.

"Mr. Jacks!"

David glanced back. The lumbering form of Martha's brother was coming down toward him. Dry weeds were crunching with every step he took. When the old man hesitated, David sighed and stood up. His eyes were bloated and achy, as if he had been crying, but he couldn't remember if he had. He rubbed them and dried the bandage on his finger with his shirt.

"Mr. Jacks?"

"Here."

The old man climbed down to him.

"You gone fishing?"

David didn't catch on for a moment.

"Oh, yeah. It's a pretty creek."

"Come late summer."

"Everybody getting along again?" David asked.

"Those two. I suppose they are. Beats me why it goes on like it does. They used to be thick as thieves. Could've been that boy Kathy hooked up with. Martha didn't take to him too well. You didn't know him, did you?"

"No. You're going to have your hands full if I leave her here."

"Martha said something like that. This family has always made do. We'll survive it. Old Missy usually gets exactly what she sets her mind to. She'll get where she's going without you. They've laid out some cold cuts and made coffee."

"I didn't want to nose in."

"No sense in turning back now."

They walked up the trail slowly. With the old man leading the way and limping badly, David had to pause several times to avoid stepping on his heels.

"You just do that?"

"It comes and goes. Fell in a gopher hole a couple of days ago."

They reached the porch. Swinging at the bugs around the light, the old man scraped his heavy feet on the mat and went in. David copied him. The living room was dark and empty. The wallpaper, the sofa and tables, and the lamps and pictures were all dry with age. A path in the carpet ran to the bright kitchen beyond and to an old woman in a frayed housecoat who was waiting with a coffeepot in her hand. She grinned and motioned him to the table. Kathy was sitting with Lisa on a couch across the room, helping her unwrap the present she had given her. There was no sign of Martha. Once their cups were filled, the old man proceeded to pour off the top of his into a wooden bowl and blow on it.

"Cools it good," the old man said.

148

David did the same thing with the bowl that had been set out for him. The coffee tasted like the inky mud they made at the print shop. He was forking some lunchmeat on to his plate when Martha appeared. She had repaired her makeup and hair. Joining them at the table, she squinted at them and touched the corner of her eye.

"I need some things out of the trailer."

"Let the boy eat, Missy."

"I just wanted to know if he was willing to lend a hand."

"Why don't you try asking him?" the old man said.

"Well?"

David's pant leg was being pulled. Lisa was beside him holding up a bikini-clad Barbie doll for him to see. He touched the doll's hair and acted as if he were enchanted by it.

"She's real pretty."

Lisa smiled and ran back to her mother. David looked up at Martha's expectant face.

"All right."

"Is there a way into the trailer?" she asked her brother.

"The screen comes off the window at the far end easy. All you need is a stepladder. I went in right after it tumbled to see how much damage there was. I took the TV out to use when ours went bad, but it didn't work neither."

"So where is it?"

"At the repair shop in town."

"Get me the claim check. I want to take it with us."

The old man got up clumsily and went into the living room.

Martha asked the old man's wife for a pencil and paper. The woman brought it with the coffee pot to refill David's cup. She sat down with them.

"I'll write down where things are supposed to be, but if they're not there, you'll have to look for them."

David nodded.

"Is there anything else you'd like?" the old man's wife asked him. "Some ketchup to make a sandwich?"

"This is fine."

"If you see anything else you think we might need, you could bring it along too," Martha said, handing him the list. "I'd go with you if I thought I could climb in and out of that window."

"You could if you had to," David said.

"I was hoping I wouldn't have to."

"I don't know if I'd be much help either," the old man said from the doorway. He handed the slip of paper to Martha. "I could probably stand outside so's you could hand things out."

"I can't do it!" Lisa said loudly.

All the heads at the table turned.

Kathy had taken the doll from her and finished putting on its dress.

"I don't know why you bought her that," Martha said. "She's too young. Every time she wants to play with it, I'm going to have to help her."

"Would that be so bad?" Kathy asked.

"You try being a mother and see how much time it takes."

"I am her mother."

"A real one."

"That's not fair."

"What? You running off up here so you can fool around with your men friends and stay out all night? You never spent any time with her when you were there. George and I were the only parents she's known."

Kathy stood up. Her fists were clenched.

"You didn't object when I was the only one putting food on the table. The truth was you couldn't make us any money 'cause nobody wanted you."

"I've never sold my wares!" Martha said.

David got up, stuffing the list into his pocket. The piece of bread rolled up with lunchmeat inside was still in his hand and he looked as if he were about to pound it on the table like a gavel. The two women paused. They were watching his bread. He flushed in embarrassment.

"You..." he said to the old man. "You got a flashlight?"

"I'll get him the lantern," Kathy said.

She was on her way to the back door. The old man got up again.

"You'll need a hand."

"I'll help him," Kathy said.

The old man looked at David and shrugged.

"You coming?" Kathy asked from the open door.

David followed her out.

"There's a stepladder in the back of the shed," the old man hollered after them.

They stopped at a small frame building next to the house. She found the lantern right away and lit it, and then held it up over the tumble of junk and rusting tools. Touching and peering wasn't producing the ladder, so she worked up her courage to move one of the boards that was obviously in the way. She dropped it quickly and jumped back.

"There's too many snakes for me," she said.

"I can probably climb in on my own."

"Good." She turned to him.

"You don't have to help," he told her. "If you want to spend time with Lisa, I can take it from here."

"No."

She ushered him out and closed the wooden latch on the door.

"We can go around this way," she said, handing him the lantern. "You first. Walk slow and make plenty of noise."

They crossed through the weeds back to the front yard. When the trail joined the twin ruts of the drive she came up to walk beside him.

"I didn't see any," he said.

"You weren't looking. You from New Orleans?"

"Indiana, near the Ohio River."

"How'd you end up down there?"

"I don't know. It seemed like it was a straight line south. And I thought it was on the Gulf of Mexico. I was going to sit on the beach and think."

"I'm crazy too," she said, smiling real big.

"You've been here a while?"

"Since... too long."

"You could probably drive Martha the rest of the way to Nashville if you wanted."

"Now there's a thought." She chuckled.

"You could see more of Lisa."

"Don't talk about something you don't know nothing about."

"Sorry," he said. They had reached the trailer. "I didn't mean to pry."

"You were being friendly. I shouldn't snap so."

David slid down the embankment. The loose soil rolled away before his feet and tumbled toward the sound of the creek below. He kicked a hole in the dirt to set the lantern up and then slid the window open. Turning to give Kathy a hand down, he found her already beside him.

"You first," he said, holding his hands out in a cradle for her foot.

She bolstered herself by grabbing his shoulder and went up. Averting his face didn't prevent the sense of her breasts going by, but as she was quickly inside he couldn't be tempted to help her further. He passed the lantern through the window.

"What's keeping you?" she asked.

"You've got to get out of the way."

He grabbed the sill and jumped, pulling himself up by stiffening his arms, but lost his balance and fell back to the ground. He tried again, this time tumbling forward with the girl pulling at his shoulders and then at his belt. The aluminum sill scraped his knee. Rubbing the sore spot, he got to his feet.

"Smells like something died in here," he said.

They were in what was left of a bedroom. Despite the jumble of overturned furniture between them and the wedge of a doorway, the floor, or wall, was only slightly tilted. The window at their feet had shattered and glass and dirt were strewn toward the bottom of the incline. David pulled the list from his pocket and held it up to the light.

"Looks like most of the stuff is in the kitchen," he said.

"You dropped something." She bent to pick up the crumpled paper. He reached for it immediately, but she had backed away and began unfolding it.

"Hey!"

He wanted to snatch the letter from her, but felt disconcerted and out of balance. She was the only other upright thing in the room.

"That's none of your business." She read it and handed it over without comment. "You always so nosy?"

"She can't spell too well."

"She never could."

Kathy was smiling.

"Fuck you," David told her.

He took the lantern and started across the high side of the room with it at eye level, afraid that he might ignite the carpet on the wall above his head.

The hall beyond the doorway was narrow, and sideways there was barely crawlspace. He set the lantern inside and climbed after it on his hands and knees. The wall creaked with every move, so he advanced cautiously. He maneuvered around the top of a closed door and waited for Kathy to catch up. He was about to tell her not to put her weight on it, but she was already scrambling across. The door swung open under her legs. He grabbed her arm and pulled her free of the hole.

"Thanks. This is getting to be like that movie about the ship that turned upside down."

"I don't think we'll drown," David said, turning to go on.

"Barring everything else, Mama's going to have a hell of time getting the scuff marks off these walls."

"I can't figure out how your uncle got that television out through here."

"So how old is this girlfriend of yours? She sounds really young."

"You're the only other person in the world that's seen that letter."

"So?"

"So it's private."

"How old is she?"

"Two years older than me."

"Really? You meet her in New Orleans?"

"I grew up with her."

"On the farm?"

"Yeah, we slopped the hogs together."

"Is that what they call it in the country?" she asked.

"Are you really a prostitute?"

"Did Mama tell you that?"

"No. Some old man who lived in the building."

"He should know."

They had reached the living room. David jumped down and almost fell because one foot landed on an end table that rocked. Taking the lantern from the ledge of the doorway above, he started making his way through the jumble. This room was in worse shape than the bedroom. With each step glass crunched beneath his feet. Shards of wood protruded from the broken furniture at every turn.

"Hey!"

He looked back and found her still sitting in the doorway. Returning, he set the lantern aside and helped her down. Instead of jumping, she edged off into his arms and held on to him until she slid free to the floor.

"I've never much cared what people thought of me," she said. "Fuck them if they can't take a joke, you know?"

In this odd light, with shadows cast upward across her face, she looked exotic. Her nose and lips were a bit too large, her eyes too widely set. Not exactly pretty, but sensual. Rather than talk to him directly, she would avert her face and make it seem as if she were watching him slyly from the corner of her eye. He thought of the photograph he had seen of her and George and wondered if this was the same woman. The other face, straight on and in bright light, had been clear and happy. Is this what death does? He had a sudden awareness of how small she was and with each closer look how she was shrinking more.

"How tall are you?" he asked.

"It all equals out."

"Don't you start."

"Start what?"

David turned away and began making his way back across the living room.

"Start what?" she asked again.

"Start whatever you think you're starting."

"What did I do?"

"You were coming on to me."

"Is that bad?"

"And if I don't want it?" he asked.

"I don't recall making an offer."

"Good."

"I don't even recall considering it," she said.

He was ignoring her. The space between the cabinets and bar, which formed a doorway into the kitchen, was blocked by dinette chairs. Untangling the legs was worsened by the electric cord and macramé that was entwined about them like creeper vines.

"You could help," he said. He held up a chair so she could pull the cord free.

"You can't even talk to a guy without him thinking you want his body."

"The whole world has been coming on to me lately."

"What are you? God's gift?"

"George's brother."

"Well, you could be, I suppose," she said.

"He must have been something."

"He was worse than all of them put together."

The chairs began coming apart.

"It doesn't look like he had it so bad."

"He's dead."

David looked at her, realizing, remembering who he was talking to. The police were after her. She had been driving the car.

"What?" she asked.

"I don't want to be George's brother."

"That's fine by me. Be whoever you want."

"We should get this over with," he said.

"All right."

He yanked out the two remaining chairs.

The kitchen was chaos. In the center of the floor a large dinette table sat upside down atop a pile of everything one could imagine coming from the cabinets and drawers: broken dishes, pots and pans, canned food and sacks and containers of flour, sugar, coffee and spices all mixed in a mound that resembled a trash heap of sand. The table gave way a bit with a scrunch when he stepped out on it, but otherwise seemed stable. He tried rocking back and forth. Nothing moved.

"The Silver Surfer," she said from the doorway.

"Wait there. I'll pass the stuff out."

He opened the broom closet and its contents fell out around him. Retrieving a tool box, he pushed the rest, a broom and mop, paint cans and potting soil off the table so he could get to the cabinet behind. The rusty pot-shaped gas attachment was where it should be as well. He handed his finds to Kathy.

"What's this thing?"

"It's for hooking up a gas line to the trailer," he said distractedly. He was going through the remainder of the cabinets. She stepped out on to the table behind him.

"What else?"

"Well, there's supposed to be a clock, which I don't see. Dishes that I think are all broken. And silverware."

She peered at the mess beneath the table.

"Here's the silverware," she said.

"Shit."

"I'll get them." She got down on her stomach and started picking forks out of the flour.

"I'll go back and get the stuff that's supposed to be in the living room."

"No, you won't. We've only got one lantern."

"I'm not thinking too clearly."

"Take a break. You've got to be tired," she said.

David sat down in the doorway, as far from her as possible, and stretched his legs out across the tabletop.

"George was a lot like a Silver Surfer," she said, hoisting up an empty drawer to hold the forks and knives. "I never did find out what happened after I left. I never saw the body. Sometimes I think maybe he's still out there somewhere sailing along. You know, like the whole thing was a big mistake. That's why I acted the way I did when you showed up."

David lit a cigarette.

"A friend of mine had been in the bar where he got hit. When she found me and told me, the only thing I could think was to get the hell out of there – that they'd probably be after me too. There were some greasy old Italians that had been trying to take a cut of what we were making. As if there was anything to take a cut of. Did Mama tell you anything about what happened?"

"The cops are looking for you and the car we're driving," David said quietly.

"Oh shit! They think..." She stopped and examined his face. "You think that too."

"I don't know."

"I didn't kill George."

She waited in vain for a response.

"Well, say something, goddamn it!"

"You don't look like a murderer."

"God!" She got to her feet. "You try so hard to believe something – it just doesn't work, does it? Why did you have to show up here? Why couldn't you just let me go on pretending?"

"Pretending George is alive?"

"You don't know, do you? Give me a cigarette." Her hand was trembling when she bent to light it from his match. "Are you lovers?"

"My girlfriend and I?"

"You and Mama."

"No!"

"But she's been snuggling up to you."

"Well... I don't know. She's confused. She's grieving for George and what's happened to her family."

"That's a good one."

"She's been through a lot."

"You don't know the half of it."

"What are you talking about?" he demanded.

"George was kind and sensitive and quick to smile. When you were with him, things were all right. He would just wrap those long arms around you and make you safe and warm all over. That's what she's grieving. The rest of us could go hang. He needed a whole lot of love, more than anybody I've ever known. Some men with that kind of need would get mealy-mouthed or turn mean. His way was to give out love in bushels – to everyone." She giggled. "He just didn't know when to stop."

"I don't believe you."

"Oh? It sounds like you've already met a few of them. He had men friends and women friends and sometimes he even turned tricks with me. Nobody was too good to sleep with – even my mother."

Her eyes darted around the room. Finally, she gazed up at the cigarette smoke floating above their heads and sighed in an odd gasping way.

"I didn't mind. Really. I loved him."

Her eyes were brimming.

"He couldn't stop. I knew he couldn't." Her voice was on that edge between laughing and crying. He hoped she wouldn't laugh – it would have to sound crazy. "I mean, I was out turning tricks, wasn't I? What was hard, the real pits, was watching her try to take him over, like he belonged to her now just because he fucked her a few times."

David didn't want to hear any more. He knew she was telling the truth. Something had been wrong from the very start. The lies to the police, the thing upstairs that came on to him, and the way Martha forgot his name. Not to mention what had happened on the highway. His pretending had been no better. What had he expected to gain by being blind? He suddenly felt queasy. He had kissed the woman for God's sake! She had been nice to him. He had just met this girl and he believed her? The whole thing was too crazy. He didn't want any part of it.

"I hope you all have a good life," he murmured.

"What?"

"I'm gone as soon as the sun comes up. Your family is too nuts for me."

"Please don't."

"After what you've told me?"

"She's threatened to file for custody of Lisa. If she's stuck here and we fight, she'll probably do it."

"I didn't hear her say anything like that."

159

"I answered the phone when she called my uncle last week. With her having custody she won't let me see Lisa at all."

"She knew you were here all along."

"You've got to take her on to Nashville."

"No. This isn't my problem."

"Think about Lisa a minute. You care about her. I know you do. You want her to grow up with my Mama as her only parent? You must have seen the way she treats her."

"It sounds like that's what will happen anyway."

"No. Listen. I'm getting some money together and as soon as I'm able I'm going to get a place where Mama can't find me. Then I'll go up for a visit and grab Lisa and run. But it won't work unless she thinks she's got me under her thumb. Don't you see, if she's the least bit suspicious she won't let me near her."

"Why don't you just tell her she can't take Lisa with her when she leaves?"

"Oh sure. After what you told me, all she'd have to do is call the cops. And she'd probably tell them some cock and bull story about you helping me to get out of New Orleans."

"You're as sorry as I am."

"It'd be just one more day with her."

"I'm not promising you."

"I could return the favor."

"You don't have anything I need," David said.

"I might." Her hands moved up to the open collar of her flannel shirt. Slowly, she began to undo the buttons.

"Stop."

"You sure?"

He looked away from the exposed skin between her breasts.

"I'm sure."

"You must love your girlfriend a lot. Not too many guys would pass up a freebee."

"Something like that."

"Well, how about a back rub. I could at least do that. You must be stiff from driving."

"That's all right. I'm fine."

"Come on, silly. I promise not to touch anything I'm not supposed to."

David didn't move.

"You have to turn around or lie down," she said, taking his hand.

He came down from the doorway and stretched out across the table on his stomach. Pulling his shirttail free, she ran her hands up underneath the cloth. Her fingers were cold and electrified.

"You're not used to being touched," she said.

"No."

"Relax. You're as stiff as a board. I won't hurt you."

He tried to do what she asked.

"What's your girlfriend like?"

"I don't know. Shy... and beautiful... and smart in a way."

"She tall?"

"About five ten."

"They grow them big back on the farm."

"She's a Swede."

"Probably has got beautiful boobs too."

"I suppose."

"And great hair, probably long and blonde. The picture of the healthy milk maiden."

"It's sort of reddish blonde. She's not real healthy. She's skinny and pale. Her parents won't let her do much because of her eyes."

"You're disappointing me. Here I thought you were in love with the perfect woman. She's at least a good fuck."

"I don't know."

"You're in love with her and you haven't fucked her?"

"I didn't say I was in love with her and I didn't say we made love."

161

"What will you admit?"

"Fuck you."

"You're a real sweet guy."

"Can't you talk about something else?"

"I'll see if I can think of anything."

They were quiet. He couldn't relax at all now. Her way of asking questions angered him more than the questions themselves. Who was she to be laughing at anyone? That bright morning in the barn with Caroline had been the clearest thing he had ever known. It hurt in comparison with his life now. Sure he was naive. Stupid too probably. But that didn't give her any right to make fun of the way he felt. Her version of love was sick. How could she think what she had was any better? She was a whore that had fallen in love with a pimp.

He shouldn't have opened his big mouth. Despite what he knew about her, there could be something he could say that she might understand. Her grief was real. She was missing all of George. Much as he was missing Caroline. If only she hadn't been so fucking cynical. She probably thinks we were a fairy tale come true – what kids believe in. What she would envy. Why should she believe she had it easier just because of the time they had together? She might be touching him, massaging his back, but he might as well be dead too. The distance between them was too far.

He didn't really want to give in to her hands, but he couldn't help himself. He was too tired. His arms, somehow disconnected, felt as if they were floating away without him. The weight of his fatigue descended, drew his eyelids closed and numbed his thoughts. Soon he was sleeping without dreams. When he awoke, he was immediately aware that she had stopped massaging his back. His shirt had been pulled down to cover the skin. He forced his eyes open. She was sitting beside him, smoking one of his cigarettes.

"How long did I sleep?"

"Just a few minutes."

He sat up and rubbed his face.

"Well, we'd better get this show on the road."

She bent forward to kiss him.

He was startled, but he didn't resist. Her lips were gentle and timid at first. This didn't last long though. He could feel the heat rise in her as if she were an oven just turned up. She pressed against him. Her tongue was exploring his mouth. Finding his hand, she drew it to her breast. David was frightened. He wasn't sure what he was supposed to be doing. Was this how it should feel – like you're being eaten alive? Her breast was heaving under his hand. She came up for air.

"What –" he gasped.

Pulling his head down to her bosom, she yanked open the remaining buttons on her shirt and wiggled free of it as she held his face to her nipple. He sucked at her and reached for the other breast with his free hand.

"The metal thing doesn't feel good," she said.

He removed the hand, certain that she would get dissatisfied with him shortly and push him away. He couldn't believe where he was or what he was doing.

His doubts were quickly dispelled when she reached for his crotch and began rubbing. This was driving him crazy. He never could have imagined anyone so hot. Her hand was fumbling with his belt buckle and then his zipper. His stiff penis was out in her hand. She was pulling at it. The thin edge of all his tense muscles, aching back and sore heart rose before he could think and burst suddenly. He wanted to scream but clenched his teeth. She continued to rub, with the goo running down over her fingers, and the explosion became pain. He grabbed her hand.

"I'm sorry," he whispered.

"It's all right. Now you can go slow."

She kissed him and from his mouth moved down, opening his shirt, nuzzling the hair there before continuing on to run her tongue along his inner thighs. As she began to lick up the melting semen, he could feel himself growing softer. If he could have willed it up again, he would have, but nothing was helping. Her mouth over the tip just made him more anxious. She was going to get real frustrated with him.

He pulled her up to lie beside him.

"You don't like that?" she asked.

"I think I need to rest for a minute."

She pecked his cheek and sat up to pull her shoes, jeans and panties off. Helping him with his, she came back to lie in the crook of his arm. David felt smothered. He was ready to move away, smoke a cigarette, anything, but he couldn't tell her. It would seem insulting. Beginning again by kissing his collarbone, she was soon up on one arm, biting his ear. Couldn't she stop moving?

"I'm not used to somebody like you," he said.

"Should I be more passive?"

He looked into her eyes for the very first time.

"No."

"I'm not good at passive." She held her breast up. "What do you think? Are they as nice as your girlfriend's?"

They were more pointed and the aureoles were much larger and darker.

"They're beautiful."

"You didn't answer my question."

"How do I get out of this?"

She straddled his leg.

"You can't. There's no rest for the wicked."

She swept her nipples lightly over his chest and moved against his leg. He felt a stirring, but he didn't know how to go on with it or what to do for it.

She licked his nipple and then began to suck. He was getting aroused.

"That feels strange," he said.

"You have hang-ups?"

"I don't know."

She came up to kiss him and moved his hand to her clitoris.

"Slowly. Gently."

He was growing hard against her belly. They were soon moving with each other. When he was sure, when his doubts were washed away by his passion, he rolled her over on her back. She helped him find his way in.

"Easy."

She was small. He held himself off for a time, letting her gradually take him. She suddenly screamed, writhed beneath him and sunk her teeth into his shoulder. He stopped, startled.

"No. Don't stop," she gasped.

Beginning again, he moved faster and faster and deeper. Her hips came up to meet his. She trembled violently and moaned. He went faster and harder. He would pin her to the table and make her come over and over and over. The power rose in him like a stone demon, a mountain rising out of mud, taking him higher. She screamed and cried. She gasped.

He drove and was thunder rolling over peaks and it exploded, tearing the top of his head off, making his groin blaze with a red heat. And it was done.

He couldn't move. Her hips continued to curl, drawing him in, as if she wanted more. She seemed somewhere else. Her closed eyes, the arched neck and arms stretched out at her sides – while the rest of her body echoed the undulations of their spent passion – made her a mindless vessel or an icon changed to flesh and bone. He didn't know what she wanted. He had nothing left to give and he couldn't take this movement any longer. Slipping out, he rolled off. She turned and cuddled against his chest without opening her eyes.

"You ok?" he asked.

"Hmmm."

"Did I do all right?"

"Big." She smiled as if from a dream.

"We should get up."

She nodded into his chest and nestled closer. After a bit her breathing became light and regular and she shivered without waking. He covered her back with the flannel shirt she had discarded.

He thought of having a cigarette but didn't want to disturb her. They would have to get up in a minute anyway. Gazing up at their reflection in the black glass window overhead, it took him a moment to realize that the man's plaintive expression was his own. Was it the shadows? He tried smiling but that looked just as odd. Everything was out of kilter. The table legs set aglow by the lantern seemed the spindly legs of some kind of overturned animal whose belly accommodated nakedness. They looked exotic, like pagan children sleeping on an altar. Where had he fallen? He didn't love her. He barely knew her. The impression, the lingering taste of her lovemaking, was bitter and off balance. Her hands had been reaching for some other, she was dreaming of someone else. He had never wanted it to be like this. What had he done?

He had betrayed Caroline.

The girl's body next to his became a weight to be shunned, her leg between his a burden. Her stringy hair, which he had ignored before, smelled of sweat and dust. Disentangling himself so as not to wake her, he searched his clothes for a cigarette and got up. He found Caroline's letter and unfolded it and read it, searching the same words over and over until her scrawl seemed nearly meaningless. Only the word "home" remained. Was that an institution, a home for unwed mothers or a hospital to kill it?

She's probably already gone. He shouldn't have sent the postcard. This piece of paper wouldn't exist. The girl on the table stirred. Hastily folding the letter, he put it back in his pants lest she discover him reading it. He had been discovered enough.

"What?" Kathy asked, startled awake by his absence.

"She knew all along!" David blurted.

Kathy sat up and rubbed her eyes.

"What are you talking about?"

"My mother! She knew about the baby!"

"Are you sleepwalking?"

"Forget it. Let's get out of here. I don't like it here."

"Wait. You're all upset. What's going on?"

David looked at her. He couldn't bring himself to say anything else, it would all sound stupid. He was being silly.

"Your girlfriend is pregnant?"

He nodded.

"Oh." She yawned. "I'm sorry. Did I do anything wrong?"

"No," he lied.

"Why don't you come talk to me about it. I've certainly spilled my beans to you."

He didn't move.

"Or you don't have to say a word if you don't want to."

There was nothing left to say. He returned to her as if he hadn't felt a thing.

Chapter Eleven

Sunlight showered them in the open loft. Beyond the rough and splintered orange floor were the meadows, the hills and the trees. And the leaves of the trees were green with the light, green with the dust blown from dry roads, green in the quiet shade. And they lay on their bellies among their discarded clothing and, elbow to elbow, they counted the ones he had climbed. She would eye him from beneath the curtain of her apricot hair with a smile that didn't believe a word he said, but would ooh and aah until he would laugh and make up something even sillier. Then he would draw her hair aside and kiss her again and wrap his arms around her to squeeze out all of the teasing. And again her skin, which glowed like the tender interior of a seashell, drew him back into the spray of dust floating in yellow air.

She was the cloud made solid, the pillow, the golden seal sleek to hold and follow. He could lay his cheek against her shoulder raised from the hair and mustard-colored straw or against her breast made firm, and hear her swell to the wave overtaking him. She was the sand. And she was as far away as the sky, her eyes the mirror of all the leaves that caught the wind. He was the climber and the swimmer, arms outstretched for the laden form just beyond reach. And then with a touch he was the fish yanked free, the bird bursting into white and she was with him, emblazoned in him like the last sudden shock of breath before the fall.

And, slickened, they would unfold from one another to dry in the sun. In silence interrupted only by the restless sparrows in the eaves of the barn, where the chicks were learning and leaving the nests, they would practice breathing slowly and might drink from their surroundings like lost children seeking a landmark. There were none. The straw itched but they didn't move. It was the call that came faintly that would bring them back. His name. And then it was repeated a little louder.

"David!"

His mother. They scrambled for their clothing. His was in the sun, in the straw. He couldn't see. She would know what they were doing if he were only half dressed. He frantically fumbled through the dense light. He couldn't see!

"David!"

* * *

He opened his eyes. The sky beyond the dirty glass overhead was light blue. It was morning and Kathy was still asleep beside him on the upside down table.

"Oh shit!"

He scrambled for his clothing. His name was called again from the other end of the trailer. He poked the girl as he sat down to pull on his shoes and socks. All she did was turn over.

"Kathy!" he whispered, as loud as he dared.

He was fumbling with his shirt buttons when a tapping noise began behind him. Turning, he found Martha peering up over the sill of the front window. Only her forehead and eyes were visible.

"What are you doing?" The glass muffled her words, but didn't disguise her anger. Luckily, the window didn't open.

"I can't hear you," he yelled and motioned for her to go around to the other end. He picked up the gas attachment as if to go meet her. Had she seen the girl? She wanted him to come to the window, but he pointed in the other direction and stepped up out of the kitchen. Counting to ten, he went back. She seemed to have gone.

"Kathy! Wake up, damn it!"

"What?"

"Your mother!"

"Oh Christ!"

She hurriedly dressed.

"Does she know I'm here?"

"I don't know."

"Well, don't just stand there. Go out and talk to her. If she asks, tell her you haven't seen me since last night."

David hesitated, and then turned and left the kitchen. He should have thanked her, but the sight of her distracted face in the daylight, much more tired and worn than the night had given hint of, had stopped him. She looked as if she would laugh at him. Tucking the gas attachment under an arm, he scrambled back through the hall with an urgency vested in her protection rather than his own. Martha called his name once more as he was climbing down into the bedroom.

"Coming," he called.

He paused, however, and took a last deep breath before going to the window. She was standing directly below with her fists on her hips. Her face was hard, her mouth set.

"Sorry," he said. "I guess I fell asleep. Is Kathy back at the house?" He handed the attachment out the window. She made no offer to accept it. "I don't want to throw it down and break it."

"Get Kathy to help you."

She quickly climbed the bank and stalked away.

"What the fuck did you expect?" he said mostly to himself. She was well out of earshot. Relieved at escaping an argument with her, he set the attachment down by the window and returned for the rest of the things in the living room. Completing their errand wouldn't count for much, but it was better than going back to the house right now. Let her stew. So what if he got caught. She had no hold on him. He hadn't made any promises. She was crazy, he told himself, but somehow he couldn't quite believe that. Had he spent too much time with her? There were parts missing. Maybe there was more to it than Kathy knew. Her mother didn't act like a murderer. She was too soft inside. Too childlike in her anticipation of his generosity.

His heart was swollen and sour with pus, ready to crack open. It wasn't as if he hadn't warned her. You'd think she would have run screaming after one good look at him. Hadn't she already had enough pain? Kathy he could understand. She was just trying to strike a bargain: trading what she had to trade to get what she wanted. Martha had come begging from the very beginning. Almost like she wanted to be hurt. She should take lessons from Kathy on how to cover her ass.

He found Kathy at the end of the crawlspace. She had put the drawer of silverware and lantern up on the ledge for him.

"Well?" she asked.

"She knows you're here. She must have seen you through the window."

"Christ! Have I screwed this..."

"Me."

"What?"

"You screwed me," David said.

"Oh. Real funny."

"I wasn't trying to be."

"Look, you had a good time. Don't make it out to be something it wasn't."

"I had a feeling what it was about," he said. "I just wanted to hear it from your sweet lips."

"I'm not getting zip, buster. So laugh it up. Hope you're having a great time."

"I'm not laughing."

"That makes two of us."

David started to tell her that her mother hadn't pushed it, that they could probably load the things into the trailer and get rid of her without a fight, but he realized he was begging the question of who would drive the damn car. He almost wanted to say he would, if for no other reason than to make her feel better. She had gone ahead without his promise to help. If only it didn't smell like blackmail. The best solution would be if Martha refused to let him near her. She was pissed off enough. He just couldn't see himself getting back behind the wheel, even if both women wanted him to.

"Maybe she'll ask your uncle to drive her the rest of the way," he said.

"That's not the goddamn point!" She shoved the drawer toward him. "Take this stuff, will you? I'd like to get out of here."

David laid the lantern atop the silverware and pushed it ahead of him as he crawled back out. By the time he had carried it to the open window, she was hopping down into the bedroom as well.

"I couldn't lift the tool box."

He would have forgotten it. Begrudgingly, he returned once more. Bringing the heavy box out quickly turned into hard work. Halfway down the hallway, he was sticky with sweat and angry with her for opening her mouth. The bedroom was deserted when he got there. He was sure she had gone back to the house. Flinging the box from the ledge, he climbed down cursing under his breath. How was he supposed to get this stuff outside? Damn her! He grabbed the box by its handle and dragged it across to the window. His finger was throbbing.

"Fuck you!"

He hurled the gas attachment out the window, and picked up the lantern.

"Hey!" came the yell from outside. He checked his throw. "Stop! You trying to brain me?"

He looked. She was cowering against the trailer.

"Sorry," he said sheepishly. "I thought you were gone."

"You need a hand, don't you?"

"Yeah."

He carefully handed the lantern down and then gave her the silverware. When he had the tool box on the window sill, he told her to move and let it drop rather than have her try to take it from him. He scrambled out and they lugged the things up to the edge of the drive.

"I'll tell your mother to bring the car up so I can load them here."

He offered her a cigarette.

"Well," she said, glancing at the house.

He looked too. The porch light had been turned off. The windows were dark.

"Yeah," he said.

They started back. She was swinging the lantern at her side.

"I wanted..." he said. "I wanted to thank you for last night."

"Hey. It was fun," she said.

He didn't know what else to say to her. In a little while he would be gone — they wouldn't see each other again. And it had been fun? That was it? He had a maddening urge to ask her to come back to New Orleans with him, but he realized it was a silly idea. The police were looking for her. And even if they didn't care any longer, what was he going to do with her? Put her in his little half-painted room. Let her go turn tricks in the evening.

"I kind of wish things were different," he said.

"If things were different we would be happy."

"What am I supposed to say?"

"Just smile. Things will get worse."

Martha had come out on to the front porch. If she saw them, she didn't let on. She carried a grocery sack out to the car and put it in the back seat. Something there occupied her until they drew near and then she turned.

"Where are the things I sent you for?" she asked.

"They're up by the trailer. If you want to drive down, I'll load them up," David told her.

She looked at her daughter.

"I'm fixing to go."

They waited.

"Are you coming or are you going to stay here?" she asked.

It took David a moment to realize she was talking to him. He glanced at Kathy.

"Well..." He felt crazy. "I guess I'll drive."

Martha tossed him the keys as if they were burning her hand. She didn't want to come near either of them. The open car door forgotten, she quickly marched back to the house.

David turned to Kathy, but found her following her mother. The screen door slammed a second time. She had to say goodbye to Lisa, he reminded himself. She had left the lantern sitting on the edge of the porch. Someone might steal it, he thought. He approached the car feeling like he wasn't moving at all. Closing the back door carefully, he opened the front and got in. This wasn't real. He played with the ignition, started the engine, and as soon as it would idle by itself he climbed out and went to sit on the edge of the porch next to her lantern.

When Martha and Lisa appeared, he started to look behind them for where Kathy would be, but changed his mind. She wouldn't see him. She would be following her daughter, waving to her from the edge of the porch. If this was to be done, it should be done quickly. He jumped up and went to the car. As soon as Lisa was settled in the middle of the front seat with her Barbie doll, he circled the yard. In a moment of weakness, he glanced up and gave a nervous wave. Her uncle was beside her scratching his forehead. She had turned. His hands were still trembling when he stopped at the pile of Martha's things beside the driveway. He looked once more after loading the trailer, but they had gone in. The house gazed back at him vacantly.

Martha was waiting. His hands were all right except for the one finger. He could drive. What happened couldn't have happened. A dream. Someone else. George was supposed to be here. His hands were white and only slightly stained with grease. They had touched everything cleanly. They had moved him here like a piece on a chess board. No one else was waiting.

He returned to the car and the estranged woman and drove them back out to the small country highway. Only Lisa seemed to be happy, quietly talking to her doll. The remaining silence felt deadly. He paused at the stop sign.

"If I turn right will that take me back to the Interstate?"

"I don't know," Martha answered. "You have to go through town anyway to pick up the television."

"It's Sunday. The shop isn't going to be open."

"It's open on Sundays. I asked my brother."

"No one in their right mind would be open this time of morning."

"The owner lives behind the shop if I remember rightly," she said. "It will take five minutes."

"All right. We'll drive by and see."

David lit a cigarette after he pulled out. He fumbled for the ashtray and missed as the highway curved around sharply. The town appeared below. On the opposite side of the little valley the sun was gleaming through the treetops.

"Don't smoke in the car. It stinks," Martha said suddenly.

He ignored her.

The streets of the town were just as quiet. Here and there, beneath the canopy of trees, kitchen lights glowed through lace curtains. A dog barked. There was a boy on a bicycle, canvas bags stuffed full with thick Sunday papers bouncing above his front tire. There was a black man sweeping the front steps of a church. Everyone else was hidden in the dark windows. Or there was no one at all. This wasn't his town. The streets had no names.

"It's right up here," Martha said.

He pulled to the curb behind a row of lifeless old cars. Martha got out. The humped back of the old Chevy in front of him made him think of those old cars his grandfather used to buy at fifty bucks a pop. An old man at his grandfather's funeral had told yet another story about his strength. They said when he was young he could lift an engine block all by himself. But David wasn't thinking of that. He saw his grandfather standing before the open door of that old car, smelling of oil and tobacco, holding a baby high over his head and grinning from ear to ear. The baby was his older brother – there was a photograph somewhere. He had stopped too soon. He didn't belong here. Martha had given up pounding on the glass and was reading the closed sign which apparently had the shop hours on it. She crossed back to the car and got in.

"They open at eight. We can go for breakfast and come back."

"I'm not waiting," he said.

He returned to the main street and started for the opposite end of town.

"Where are you going?"

"Back to the Interstate."

"Wait a minute."

"I said I'm not waiting!" he said.

"Lower your voice," she hissed.

He glanced over. Lisa had moved under the protection of her arm.

"I want to know why you can't wait an hour."

"I'm a son of a bitch."

"I asked you a civil question."

"I want to get this drive over with."

"One hour is not going to make that much difference."

"There's no guarantee the shop will open when the sign says. We could be waiting all morning."

"If he doesn't show up in an hour, we'll leave without it," she offered.

"Oh no we won't. I can hear you say, 'We've waited this long — a little longer won't hurt.' You can have your brother ship it to you if it's that important."

"How's he going to do that if I've got the claim check?"

"So mail it to him. I'm not waiting."

They had reached the entrance to the highway. David flicked the turn signal on as he stopped. The dash light clicked and clicked and clicked. He spun the wheel, taking the ramp. The signal continued to click. He flipped it off.

"All you think about is yourself!" Martha said angrily. "What do you expect me to do with Lisa up there without a television? And all because you want to get on some stupid bus to go back to some stupid job! They won't even notice you're not there!"

"Yes they will." David winced as he checked the rearview mirror.

"You're in such a hurry to get back to your little miserable life. You're fooling yourself. How could anybody be happy in that hole you're living in? Or in that job where all you get for your trouble is smashed and filthy fingers."

"You should mind your own business."

"You're unhappy 'cause you're so self-centered that nobody wants to be near you. You've got no friends. Your family disowned you. You don't even have a girlfriend —

how natural is that? You hang around those fairy boys. You either are one of those sick disgusting things or you like them 'cause they make you feel superior. Either way you're sick yourself. You think you're superior to everybody. Even me!"

"I've never said that," he tried to reply evenly.

"You don't have to. You've been throwing yourself around ever since we started. I've had it up to here! You're going to turn this car around and go back and do what I want you to do!"

"Forget it."

"I'm not going to forget it. You can walk back to New Orleans. Let's see how you like that, mister!"

"I'll pull over right here and get out if that will suit you!" David said loudly. He was turning red.

"You're a lousy person. You don't think I know what was going on in that trailer? You're so fired up to get to Nashville, that you had time to fool with my daughter! Here I was sitting in that house bone-tired, barely able to keep my eyes open and wondering what's happened to you. I was even beginning to worry that you hurt yourself before it dawned on me what was keeping you. It was just you thinking about yourself again."

"Shut up."

"I will not. You've been making up to me and Lisa like butter wouldn't melt in your mouth and now you're doing this. You do get whatever you want, don't you. I bet it was the same way with that dumb girl you had back home. Boy, was I a chump. I don't mind being a fool so much, but did you have to make Lisa into one too? She was really beginning to open up to you. She'll know the truth now. You don't think enough of her to make a delay to get the television for her. It sure takes a real man to mistreat a little girl. You must be proud of yourself."

"You shut up!" David screamed. Martha and Lisa cringed. "Not one more word! I swear I'll kill you. I've had enough of your bullshit!"

He couldn't see the highway, he couldn't see anything. His heavy foot pressed the pedal further, rushing them head-on into oblivion. His breathing was shallow. Silent. The steering wheel would not yield to his stranglehold. He dared not look at her. She had tried to use Caroline against him! And she didn't even realize what she was doing. He would kill her for that. None of the rest was important. She was the stupid and self-centered one. She didn't even know. Then, as if his trapped fury were being leaked off by some insidious and mute whistle, the blinding pressure in his forehead began to lessen. He should hold on to it, revel in it, but that was impossible. She would try to trick him again and he wouldn't be able to resist. Wasn't he stronger now, didn't he understand what she was doing? He had frightened her. No, the anger didn't matter. He wouldn't be used any longer. He was through giving – he understood. Nothing he could do would make her be kind to him.

He could chance looking at them now. He was in control. Martha averted her face when he turned and apparently gazed out the side window at nothing in particular. Her eyes peeked back at him from the dim reflection of her face in the glass. Frightening her may not have been such a bad thing, he thought. Lisa was snuggled closely at her side, with a thumb stuck in her mouth and the other hand twisting a strand of her own hair. Her eyes were wide and anxious and wouldn't hide. He had to retreat.

He checked his speed and the empty highway. Of course she couldn't understand. All she knew was that he had shouted at her grandmother. She couldn't see his frustration or the screwed reasons for what went on around her. It must be terrible being small and lost in the sea of adult arguments. There wasn't anything he could do to make it up to her. At the next exit, he slowed and moved into the right hand lane. Out the corner of his eye, he caught Martha turning to him, but she waited to speak until he had crossed the overpass and had entered the highway on the other side, going back the way they had come.

"You changed your mind?" she asked.

"Yes."

The ride back to town went quickly. The exit came. The tumbling, rolling road ran down through the thick pine and up again to the same little grocery store and post office. Everything was closed and quiet except for the church. Cars were in the lot and families were slowly strolling toward the steps and front door. One lady was holding her hand against the new sun. They turned off and found the shop. When he parked, he noticed that one of the old cars was missing. This was all very reasonable. Only the open shop, with its door agape on an early Sunday morning, seemed odd. They got out and crossed the street together. Inside was a small burly man leaning over the counter where he had the Sunday funnies spread. He was sipping coffee. Martha dug into her purse and produced the claim stub.

"This one's been ready some time," he said, turning. "I was beginning to wonder if it was mine to keep."

He returned with the large television and set it atop the newspaper.

"You like working Sundays?" David asked.

The man gave Martha the receipt.

"Don't like to fish." He leaned across the counter to Lisa. "Hello missy. I reckon you can watch Popeye again, huh?"

Martha glowered at David. He grabbed the set and carried it out and across to the trailer. They were close behind. Martha waited as he opened the doors and loaded the television. He was sure she would have something to say about the way he was rearranging the boxes and was ready to bite back, but she didn't offer her opinion. Lisa had pulled free of her grasp and was examining a nearby bush. Once he began locking up, Martha returned to the car and called the little girl. She didn't respond immediately, apparently preoccupied with whatever she had discovered. David stepped over to her. There was a big caterpillar on a leaf before her.

"That's a caterpillar," he said. "It's going to change —"

Her terrified glance stopped him. She ran for her grandmother who welcomed her with open arms. Martha hugged her and smiled vindictively.

Chapter Twelve

The air rose from the hood in thick waves, twisting and buckling the reflection of the car wash sign in the windshield. This was the dying reverberation, an hour's ride with a rumbling knocking engine. Sweat dribbled down David's eyebrow and streaked his cheek. His fingers were scorched reaching into the front grill for the release lever and he jumped back waving them painfully. The hood was still down.

"There's a rag next to the pump," the boy shouted to him.

The cloth was draped on the side of a bucket of soapy water. He wet it and went back. When the hood popped up a swell of blistering heat hit him full in the face. There was nothing to be touched. The radiator cap might explode with steam to burn his hand again. He stepped back and wiped his forehead with the damp cloth.

"Looks like you got a little problem," the boy said at his shoulder. "Could you move it to the side of the building? There's a water hose there you can use."

David nodded and climbed back in the car. The engine sputtered, knocked a few times and then died. He tried again, letting the engine grind. Nothing.

"Goddamn car!" He hit the steering wheel with both hands.

The boy was at the car window.

"You'll have to push it out of the drive. I've got a line up here."

"All right!" He turned to Martha. "You're going to have to steer."

Jumping out, he went to the rear bumper, positioned his feet and shoved with all his might. The car rocked a little, but didn't budge. He tried with his back against the trunk. This time it didn't even rock. He turned around and tried once more putting everything he had left into forcing it to roll forward just an inch. He didn't care any longer about moving it. He wasn't going to be beaten by a fucking car. When the muscles in his neck seized up, he quit. The boy came back.

"If you can't move it, I'll have to have it towed out of the drive. You'll have to pay a towing charge."

"Give me a minute, will you!"

David shooed Martha over and got back behind the wheel to try the key again. The ignition churned and churned. Finally, on the third attempt, the engine turned over. It was still knocking violently. He shifted into Drive and suddenly realized where he had found the stick.

"Did you have this in Park the whole time I was pushing?" he demanded.

"You didn't say a word about changing it," Martha said.

"Christ!"

He pulled around to the side of the station. Out and running as soon as he stopped, he grabbed paper towels from the open men's room and yanked the hose back to the car. Steam burst from the radiator cap when he loosened it. After a moment the cap could be removed. Even with the hose on full blast the radiator seemed to take forever to fill. The knocking grew quieter and he went back to turn the spigot off.

"Leave it running!" he shouted to Martha, as he headed for the front of the building. He found who he thought was a mechanic. The man was settling a bill with another customer.

"I've got a problem with my car. Can you come take a look?"

"Be right with you."

"It's overheating. I'm afraid to leave it running very long."

"I'll be over in a sec." The man turned to his cash register.

David returned to the car to wait. The knocking could be heard from the corner. It was as loud as ever. Martha was standing next to the open hood, amidst the clouds of steam rolling off the engine, looking as if she was about to tear her hair out.

"What are you doing?" she demanded.

"The mechanic's coming."

"Where is he? Get him!"

David went back again. The mechanic was under the hood of another car. He glanced up and reached for a rag to wipe his hands.

"All right."

He followed David this time. The knocking was louder than before.

"Unhook the trailer and bring it around to the garage," the mechanic told him. "Hurry. You're burning your engine up."

Scrambling for the trailer hitch, David pulled the chains and the brake lights loose and lifted the trailer free from the ball. He jumped behind the wheel as Martha pulled Lisa out. The car chugged and shuddered, but made it to the front of the station. Shutting it off next to the mechanic's bench was a blessed arrival. The silence was easy.

He rested at the wheel for a moment, feeling as though there had to be one more thing to do, but he couldn't think of what it might be. The mechanic could ask him to start the car again — he had done that for his grandfather and father when he was a boy — although the longer he sat there the less likely it seemed he was needed. Upon remembering that, as a child, he had been sorely tempted to blow the horn in his father's face, he grinned to himself and climbed out. He stopped in the office for a soft drink and held the bottle, its edges worn white from too many washings, against his forehead as he went out to find Martha and the child. They were sitting on a picnic table near the trailer. Martha shook her head at him when he offered the bottle.

"All right for Lisa to have some?" he asked.

"She's had enough sweets to last a week."

"How about some water?" he asked the little girl.

She shook her head as well.

"So what's wrong with the car?" Martha asked.

"He's working on it now."

"You ask him what he's doing?"

"Trying to find the problem."

"So it could take him the rest of the day."

"How should I know?" David said.

"Watch Lisa. I'm going to call my brother and have him come get us."

"You might wait and see. He might find it right away."

"Why can't you think? What are we supposed to do when the sun goes down?"

She walked away. Once she was out of sight, David offered the soda to the little girl. She wanted to hold the bottle, but he insisted on helping, afraid that she would spill it. She gulped the liquid as if she were dying of thirst.

"You tired? You want to lie down and rest?" he asked.

Lisa shook her head. She wouldn't look at him.

"This morning, I wasn't mad at you — you know?"

Her face was haggard and her eyes bleary. He wanted to pick her up in his arms and comfort her, and would have if he didn't expect her to protest. Nothing could seem fair to her. She didn't understand why she was awakened again and again and made to sit in uncomfortable places. Or why everyone was yelling at each other. Almost as if she were reading his mind, her face began to crumble with the misery of her weariness. Tears ran down her cheeks. David put a hand on her shoulder. She shuddered and scooted away.

"I want to go home," she said.

"It won't be much longer. I'll get you there."

"Will Mama be there?"

"She wants to be," he said, unable to think of anything better.

"I want my Mama."

She began crying in earnest. He reached for her, but she flailed against his hands.

"Hey..." he said softly.

Martha brushed by him and gathered her up. Nestling the child's head in the crook of her neck, she turned on him.

"What did you do to her?"

"She's just tired."

"I'm taking her to the car," she said, carrying her off. "It's all right, Missy. We'll get away from the bad man. You don't have to cry now."

If she had intended to hurt him with that remark, she had succeeded. Lisa would believe her. Why shouldn't she? Martha was the center of her universe. What had he been thinking? His anger had only played out the losing hand he had been dealt. It was her cards, her deck, her table and chairs. She was the house. He wearily stretched out on the picnic table and looked up at the blue sky. In a moment someone was nudging him. He awoke groggy, unable to remember closing his eyes. The mechanic was standing beside him.

"Found your problem. There's a leak where the hose attaches to the bottom of the radiator."

"How long will it take to fix it?"

"Two hours at most."

"All right."

After the man left, David forced himself up. He should tell Martha even if she didn't deserve the time of day. It was her car. She was at the water fountain in the office.

"He just told me," she said as soon as she saw him. "This is my brother's number. Call him and tell him not to come."

The slip of paper trembled in her hand. He took it.

"You are a bitch," he said softly.

She turned and went into the garage. "I'm taking a nap," she said.

"Too tired to fight," he muttered.

* * *

Wind, with its mouth gaping, sweeps down the dark alley, brushing by the man on the last step and the car that awaits him. His hair is ruffled, the car antenna wavers. On the pavement between them, a newspaper soaked by the rain flaps once limply. Laughter whispers from a window above and somewhere a shutter slams. Water drips and drips like the patter of another, smaller, animal racing over tile. He will turn his collar to the damp air. Had Martha been invited, she would have turned it for him. And when he steps down his feet will echo. Headlights burst over him. His white face will look up to the glare rushing for him. Tires are squealing. The black car will smash him, send him sprawling over the hood and into the windshield.

His face will burn there, searing flesh will slide over glass, unconscious eyes will stare and then smear in their rapid arc to death. Forehead and nose will flatten. Lips, which once kissed with a breath both sweet and stale, will be crushed, bone and teeth will shatter and rent the skin. The scream that never came, will come later, with the tires screeching to a halt. The rain returns in sudden waves to shock and chill and every trace is washed away. In its mist his body becomes a shadow or a puddle on the pavement. And she begins again, searching through the streaked windshield for her lover on the steps.

Then beneath the lamp, behind the weave of downpour, the face would bow once more, a smile still on the corners of the lips, as hands turn collar against the cold. The shadow would hide the eyes and accent the forehead and long nose. And with a step down, the face will slide suddenly into darkness. Headlights flash. An engine roars and, now silently, tires spin across slickened pavement, rushing toward him. One quick thump – and metal, flesh and rain all falter in an instant before he falls, dives, swims with arms outstretched, to the crushing glass. His face rolls over the windshield and remains there.

The rain has become his face. Sheets of water running down define a brow, a nose and broken lips slipping off. With each new wave the features are erased and redrawn. And the liquid thickens and oozes. She can feel it clinging to her skin. Yet again, beyond the melting membrane of windshield, his silhouette rises before the steaming hood and awaits its fate. Metal shudders. And the swimmer slides, rushing across to her. Hands race through dissolving glass to grasp her and the face, smashed and smiling, cracked and crumbling, embraces her and sinks like a babe to her shoulder.

* * *

He found the pay phone and dialed the number. The receiver rang and rang and rang before it was answered. A woman's faint voice said hello amidst the crackling and popping of the bad connection. Shouting to make himself heard, he discovered he was talking to the brother's wife. He explained the situation to her only to find that they had sent Kathy out fifteen minutes before with the truck. There was nothing to be done. He hung up and walked back out into the sunlight. Stumbling to the picnic table, he tried to figure how long it would take her to reach them, but he couldn't think clearly enough to make up his mind. He probably wouldn't be able to stay awake to watch for her either.

Again across the hard table, with his head propped up so that he could see the traffic, he tried to doze, but couldn't. It was too soon for her to appear. He was too far from the highway to jump up and flag her anyway. They would talk for a moment and she would go. Nothing would have changed. The cars were coming one at a time as quick slashes of motion low against the trees, each signaling with the sun on glass or chrome. Their sweeping runs held the woods back like the swing of a scythe might hold tall grass at bay. The movement seemed frantic — almost not enough. The withered wrists and fingers of the trees were straining for him. When he awoke the highway was empty. The pines across the road were still. He simply looked for a while at the quiet clarity before him. The hairline texture of branches and needles against the sky, the porcelain blue, seemed the burst of a fountain caught and held or a spider's web pressed by the wind across a wall. There was an intimacy to this. And it came to him that he had been rushing for a very long time. Images which had run madly by — dried splotches of paint on the wooden floor, a finger squeaking down a guitar string, the wall of black clouds over the river, her eyes looking away as she talked, the gate lying hidden in the weeds at dawn, her breasts swinging above him in the white glare of the lantern — all threatened him and hurt him. And there were more, pressing him, drawing him back up and out like a fever that wouldn't let him think or choose for himself. This was better. He would embrace silence. The forest of his childhood was like this. He could sit among trees where the birds didn't sing and where his own breathing became the hollow distant whisper of leaves. Alone. Alone. A place where the hand lying in brown needles could be anything. Slicing it neatly at the wrist, the blood would flow gently out and never quite form a puddle. It would bubble and dissolve in the thick matting. Only faint regrets would surface. But there was a presence here, creeping over him, pulsating like his own heart's blood as it oozed out. It was growing, enveloping him. The silence was screaming, drumming in his ears, filling him with dread. The pines were still and stiff with shadows waiting horribly. He would run. He would yearn for her dark skin in the white lantern, he would cling to her for substance. She had to be there.

The sound of a pickup near the trailer roused him. He got up woodenly, relearning his heavy frame as he stepped forward. His neck and side ached from the awkward position he had been lying in. The sunlight on the windshield prevented him from seeing who was in the cab, but he waved just the same and approached the window. It was Kathy. She looked tired. Her hair, still dirty, was tied back tightly with a rubber band. She had changed clothes. The flannel shirt was a different color from the one she had on this morning.

"Hello," she said.

"You sleep any?" he asked.

"A little. You look like you could use a nap."

"So... do you still love me?"

She looked at him.

"What's happening with the car?" she asked.

"It'll be repaired in a bit. We're going on. But you could keep me company until it's ready."

"Where is everybody?"

"Asleep in the car. You didn't answer my question. You still love me?"

"Oh come on."

"Well, you want to stop?"

"If I can have a beer." She was looking past him. "That place open?"

He turned. There was a tavern next door. Above its dark cavity of a doorway was a large lettered sign reading "Girls."

"The door's open."

He tried to kiss her after she got out. She ducked.

"Don't get nuts on me. All right?" she said.

"All right," he replied, but he felt crazy. He was angry and needy; he wanted to talk stupidly, insult her, and seduce her. He couldn't get it straight.

He followed her across the hot parking lot, not daring to say any more. Stepping into the tavern was like falling into a deep well. He hesitated rather than jostle her and after a moment realized she was no longer with him. He reached out and inched his way forward, whispering her name. No one answered. Slowly the room surfaced against the darkness. She was sitting at a small table across the room. There was a stage and more tables. Here and there were men drinking beer. A waitress moved among them. He made his way to her table.

"What is this place?" he asked.

"Don't ever say I never take you anywhere."

The waitress came and returned with beers.

"How's Lisa holding up?" she asked.

"She was crying and asking for you. How did you expect her to do?"

"Thanks. That's just what I needed to hear."

"Let's take these outside," he said.

"And miss the show?"

She guzzled her beer and waved down the waitress for another.

"And a tequila shooter this time. You want one?" she asked him. "I'll buy."

He shook his head.

"Mah Lady." A man was standing over them. Only the edge of his forehead and cheek and the strap of an eye patch could be seen in the darkness. He was either thickly built or had on several layers of clothing. The hand on the tabletop was fat and the fingers were short and round like sausages. He stank.

"Gypsy!" she exclaimed. "What are you doing so far from home?"

"Gypsy wanders the whole world. Sees freends every way he turns. You have some change?"

She reached in her pocket. The waitress returned.

"Out!"

"But Gypsy talks to his freends."

"Out on your own or I get Mr. Frank."

"He can sit with us," Kathy said.

The man held up the dollar bill she had just handed him.

"I pay."

"Out. And you two can go as well if you insist."

"Mah Lady, Gypsy leaves. You stay and enjoy. Life is short."

"Fuck 'em if they can't take a joke," Kathy told him.

"You and Gypsy laugh last," he said and shuffled toward the bright doorway.

The waitress set the drinks on the table.

"Sorry to give you trouble," Kathy said. "I wouldn't have encouraged him if I'd known."

She didn't answer.

"Did you see the eye patch?" Kathy asked David after she had gone. "He told me a beautiful story one night about giving up his eye so his blind daughter could see."

"You believed him? How do you know him here?"

"You didn't get very far from my uncle's farm. He wanders around the county. He's got a graceful soul. He's my good luck charm."

She emptied the shot glass, ate the salt from her hand, and sucked the slice of lime.

"You sure you don't want one?" she asked after she set the half-empty beer mug down.

He shook his head. Music blared from the corners of the room. It sounded tinny and crackly as if the speakers were torn and repaired with glue or the turntable had a bad needle. The lights came up on stage. After a long moment, after the bass of the rock and roll seemed to thump on and on endlessly, a skinny girl appeared and began to grind.

She had made the first tentative gesture of disrobing when the song ended. Mouthing the words, as if she needed no orchestration except what was in her head, she flailed about in the silence until someone started the record again. Her fringed vest came off.

"You like this?" Kathy asked, leaning forward.

"I wanted to talk to you," he shouted.

"So talk."

He dismissed her with a curt wave of his hand.

"Don't get your dander up," she said.

The girl on the stage was taking off her halter top. Wobbling her large and droopy breasts, her tassels swung but didn't complete the full circles she seemed to be trying for. She danced toward the edge of the stage where they were sitting. The tassels hung straight down from her pasties like pull strings on a pair of closet light bulbs when she bent forward with her arms outstretched to coax David up. He shook his head vehemently. She went away.

"You don't want me," Kathy said. "You're still madly in love with that puppy dog back home."

"I don't know what you're talking about."

The music stopped. The girl took a bow to the scattered applause and whistles and then scurried off.

"I wanted you to help me forget her," he said suddenly.

"There's a thing the Arabs do to get a divorce," Kathy continued. "They go to the top of a mountain and turn around three times saying I divorce thee. If you want me, then you got to do that here and now, to prove your undying love."

"You probably think I should have got up there with that girl as well. Make a total ass of myself."

"It wouldn't hurt you."

"What do you know?"

"A lot more than you," Kathy said. "You're still in diapers."

"And you've seen it all?"

"I didn't see it on television. You know what I meant when I said 'Fuck 'em if they can't take a joke?' George taught me that. It means if a man can't laugh then he's a fucking john and he deserves to be taken."

"So what. So you're a smart whore. Big deal."

"I don't see you laughing, buddy boy."

"I'm not a john. Tell you something you don't know. Old George wasn't just screwing around with your Mama. He had a nice little thing going on with that fairy upstairs Toni."

Her face fell.

"I knew that," she said. "As a matter of fact, he told me himself. We didn't have any secrets – not one. He told me everything!"

"Whatever you say."

"Don't hand me that shit."

"I don't want to fight with you. Why don't we get out of here?" David said.

"I'm not ready to go. I'm tired of driving."

"You know, Martha's asleep in the car. I bet we could take Lisa without her waking up. You two could be long gone before she found out. I could stay and make her go on to Nashville."

"She'd be after me in a second."

"Not without a car. I've got the keys."

"It will be months before I can afford to move out of my uncle's. You might get her to Nashville, but she'd be right back down here as soon as she figured out how."

"I don't think you really want her."

"I don't want her for a couple of weeks and then have her taken away again. I won't do that to her."

"If it was me –"

"If it was you, you'd run away and never show your face again. You don't know a thing about having a child."

"Maybe not. But I can see what Lisa needs!"

"You want her, smartass!" Kathy said. "Give me a piece of paper. I'll sign her over to you. You figure it out."

"She's not mine."

"Mister High and Mighty. Where's the paper?"

She waved the waitress down and asked for a pen and something to write on and another shot of tequila. When it was delivered, she scribbled out a note and signed it with a flourish. David wouldn't accept it. She bent and stuffed it in his pants pocket. He wanted to push her away, but was afraid he would knock her off her chair and start a scene.

"Keep that in your goddamn pocket with your other promises."

"It's not worth anything," he said.

"Why don't you just pretend it's a joke? You like a good joke, don't you?"

"This isn't funny. You can't give away your daughter."

"How did you do it?" she asked, and with her nose in the air, dismissed him with a curt wave – a parody of his previous gesture.

"Hey," she said, leaning on the table, "if you had her and I came for her you'd hand her over in a second, wouldn't you?"

"I guess."

"Well, there you go. So do whatever you want."

The music interrupted them. Another girl came out to dance and strip. David watched her distractedly. How was he supposed to feel? Why should he even consider kidnapping a three-year-old? What would he do with her? This wasn't real. Any more than the girl on stage was real. As she uncovered herself, the breasts, the belly and the gyrating thighs became rubbery and unyielding, a pasty replica of flesh. The eyes of the men, some wide, others squinted and hidden in smoke, were glowing from the dark tables. This wasn't desire. It was something else that hung over them like the thick cloud in the air near the ceiling.

"You want her, don't you?" Kathy asked.

He slowly shook his head. Saying yes, falling into the dream, would have been easier.

"Think I've got the body to do this?" she asked.

"Sure. Why not."

"I used to do it for George sometimes. This might even be better. And I'd get paid for it."

"I don't know anything about taking care of a child," he told her.

"Figure it out for yourself."

She was getting sloppier by the minute.

"The more I think about it the better it gets," she said. "Everybody looks, but nobody touches. You say I could do it, right?"

He nodded.

"Maybe I should get up and audition now."

"You should talk to the owner first."

"If he saw me he'd be sure to hire me."

"You probably need to clean up and do a costume."

"Oh yeah." She looked down at what she had on and touched her ponytail. "This could be a costume. Farm girl stripper. What do you think?"

"They've got more to take off."

"You'd get up there with me?"

"No. Nobody wants to look at me. I've got to go as soon as the car's fixed. I won't be here tomorrow."

"Right now, silly. You got a nice body."

"You're drunk." He grabbed her wrist.

"I am not," she said, carefully removing his hand. "Nobody touches. I could be another what's her name... Gypsy Rose Lee. No, that won't work. Gypsy's outside. I'll be another Kathy."

"Right."

The music stopped. The girl on the stage was gone.

"George always had a thing for females. Performers. He couldn't keep his eyes to himself. Didn't matter what they were doing. I could do it as a tribute to him. In his memory like." She was gazing at the empty platform before them. "He sure did like to play-act. 'Let's pretend,' he'd say and off we'd go. Toni got it wrong. She thought it was her, but it wasn't. He just wanted to pretend. You ever been anybody else for a while? Sort of like a roller coaster – you go up and down and there's no time to think about what you would do if you were you. What did she say about him?"

"Toni?"

"Yeah, I want to know what George told her."

"All Toni said to me was that George had the soul of a poet and he was wasting his time with you and your mother. And that George had given her a song."

"A song? You remember it?" she asked.

David could see her on the stage, her nails moving, changing chords; he could hear her low voice, but not the words or the melody. He recalled grief and the pain of being left behind. Someone else's music testifying to his guilt.

"No."

"Mary Magdalene?"

"Maybe something like that," he said.

"That son-of-a-bitch!"

"I don't really remember it."

"But how you paused for that certain sound," she sang, "Of cloth murmuring on the bright floor as I stepped free..."

"It was different."

"Of course it was different. I can't sing." She looked back up at the stage. "I should've been somebody else. He just gave it away cause he wanted to hear it sung. That's some kind of joke on Toni. Her up there, singing my pregnant song. Serves her right. You gonna play with old George you'd better be ready to be something you ain't."

"I've already found that out," David muttered. "You ready to go?"

"One more for the road." And she flagged the waitress and reordered tequila and beer. David shook his head when she offered him a refill. He was still nursing his first one.

"So Toni came on to you. You sleep with her?"

"You know Toni's a guy?"

"Sure. So did you fuck her?"

"No. I don't do that. He helped me load the trailer and I went over to the club where he sang. He showed me a picture of you and George."

"Where did he get a picture like that?"

"He didn't have it. It was in the dresser we were moving. He thought I was George's brother."

"I can't stand it. Now she's going through my things. It wasn't bad enough that Mama has probably poked at everything. What else did you find to look at? My panties and bras?"

"I didn't touch anything. I only saw the picture 'cause it was laying on top in one of the drawers."

"She take anything?"

"Not that I know of."

"I wouldn't put it past her." The tequila came and she emptied it quickly. "God! They're robbing me blind. What else do they want? What am I, some kind of fucking joke? They should leave the poor dog alone."

"Calm down."

"How'd you feel if it was you? My mother is over there sleeping like a baby. She killed my boyfriend!"

"You're going to get us kicked out of here."

"You think I fucking care! You think I give a damn?"

And she was up from her chair, clambering onto the stage before he could stop her. He stood, but the distance to the top of the platform was insurmountable. The men in the audience would laugh their heads off. She was in the center now, swaying unsteadily.

"Hi!"

The room was silent.

"I'd like to dedicate this dance to all the black widows in the whole world... And a piece of advice... Never let your mother sleep with your lover... Hey, that kind of rhymes... Where's the music? Hey!" she shouted, "how about a little music!"

There was chuckling in the audience.

"What's so fucking funny? Excuse me, you go right ahead and laugh. There's plenty to laugh at. Well... if they're not going to give us a song we'll have to make our own, right?" She tapped her foot. "Because of the red flowers in the earthen jar... And the sunlight on the floor before my window..."

As she was fumbling with the buttons of her shirt, the waitress and a big guy with tattoos jumped up on the stage. They tried to take her arms. She pulled away and stumbled. Helping her up, they escorted her off at the other end. David went around the tables to meet them. The big guy plunked her down in an empty chair.

"She belongs to you?" he asked David.

"I guess."

"Then get her out."

"They've got a tab," the waitress said.

"How much?" David asked, afraid of what was about to happen. He knew he didn't have enough.

"I've got it, damn it!" Kathy said and pulled a wad of bills from her pocket. David took the money and found a twenty to give to the waitress. "This is the last time I come in this fucking joint!" Kathy went on. "Can't have fun. Wasn't like I was hurting anybody!"

"Shut up!" David said.

He grabbed her arm and got her to her feet. Almost to the door, she jerked free.

"Don't touch," she said, and then yelled back into the tavern. "I don't give a fuck, you hear me!"

He thought he might have to force her out, but she turned and staggered into the sun. The afternoon was brighter and hotter than ever. Tiny sparks of light danced across his vision as he paused to get his bearings. Kathy was nearly reeling. She had turned away and with one hand occasionally grazing the wall for support, she staggered toward the garbage cans sitting near the rear of the building. It took him a moment to understand where she was going. Gypsy was sitting on the ground against the back corner, his legs spread-eagled before him and a bottle propped at his thigh. His clothes were stained and sooty and his bare feet were black on the bottoms as if he had just been walking in fresh tar. David followed her. When she reached the man, she went down on her knees and hugged him. And then like a child seeking solace, she slid down until her head was in his lap and she could look up into his nodding face. She was confessing, communing, and muttering all the inarticulate sins of her drunkenness.

"Kathy," David called half-heartedly.

"Fuck 'em..." she was mumbling to Gypsy. "If they can't love a joke."

Gypsy stirred and patted her head.

"Kathy," David called again. He approached them cautiously. A step too close might break something. He didn't know what to do.

"Kathy. You can't stay here."

She looked up as if from a drowning dream. Her head wavered.

"My angel of mercy," she slurred. "I run away and here you are again."

He reached out a hand and she took it and he pulled her up to her feet. Sweat glistened on her forehead. Putting his arm around her, he started her back toward the filling station. She was clumsy: dead weight under his arm.

"Bye," she whispered. "Bye bye."

They made it to the pickup. He opened the door on the passenger side and helped her up. Had she been unconscious he could have left her in the cab to sleep it off, but as she seemed determined to stay awake he was afraid she might decide to drive off. She began fumbling with the glove compartment button.

"I'm going to get some coffee," he told her. "You stay put. Don't do anything until I get back. All right?"

"Sure thing."

When he returned, he found her with the glove compartment open and in a jumble, and an unfolded piece of paper in her hand. She was snorting the white powder with a rolled-up dollar bill. Another empty paper was lying open on the dash. There was a revolver and a box of shells in the glove compartment.

"A little pick-me-up," she said, offering him the bill and the powder.

"No."

She shrugged and finished.

"You want this?" he asked.

She took the coffee and blew across the top.

"So are you ready to grab Lisa and make a run for it?" she asked.

"No."

"I meant you and me."

His anger would show if he looked at her.

"I don't think you're ready to go anywhere," he said.

"You underestimate the power of a squirrel."

"Do you know what you've just done?" he asked.

Her eyes widened.

"Well, sort of. Things kind of go blurry sometimes."

A drunken roughened Martha was suddenly looking at him from her face. He turned away, repulsed.

"Who cares what I've done?" she said.

The real Martha appeared next to the taillight of the car in the open garage door. She started toward them.

"Your mother's coming," he told her.

"I'll be the perfect lady." Kathy began stuffing everything back into the glove compartment.

"Where have you been?" Martha demanded, as soon as she was close enough to be heard. "What's the idea traipsing off without saying a word? The car's been ready for half an hour!"

Kathy slammed the glove compartment and jumped from the truck.

"You're giving me a headache. Shut your frigging trap before I close it for you!" she shouted at her mother.

Martha sputtered and then turned red.

"I figured it was you! I could smell the whisky from inside!"

"Murderer!" Kathy yelled louder.

"Get in your truck and get out of here before you're sorry!" Martha said.

"You're a bitch, you hear me, a bitch! Bitch! Bitch! Bitch!"

They were drawing in toward each other. David stepped in front of Kathy and gave her a shove.

"Stop!" he said.

"Who are you to be shoving people," Kathy pushed him back but he didn't budge. "You're going to be sorry you did that, buster. You shouldn't have done that to me, you dumb fuck!"

She climbed in the truck, yanked the door shut and scooted across to the wheel. The truck started.

"Wait one second," he yelled through the window.

"You're a lousy fuck too!"

Her tires squealed from the lot and she was gone.

Chapter Thirteen

In the blazing light of the afternoon there are no darkened corners to contain his fears. Below the cracked lip of the chrome fender, below the splotches of brown floating in the glare, the pavement is simply gray or blue. The sandpaper surface runs back between the tires like a tongue left to harden in the heat. And he hesitates. Movement might shatter cold sweat or dispel this gaping madness, but that would mean joining the face behind the glass, closing the slab of door and grasping the worn plastic stick. The car beckons. It is ready. Come embrace the machine that kills.

He has already driven it mile after mile on the road that has unraveled all the hills and rocks he knew. Innocence is easily undone. Why hesitate? Crawl out of the broken shell. Wrinkled eyes, laughing behind the windshield, have promised this from the beginning. She has drawn his summer blood. And he wanted to lie with his arm across the white, white belly, rest his face on the shoulder whose skin is as dry as fallen leaves. Now climb into the seat, clammy against his back. Climb in through his cold fear. She is comfort.

* * *

After the long hill, the highway curved about the mountain to the right in an arc that surely ran beyond the low sun. Beneath his window, rows of corn swung by like the spokes in a great green wheel. And it came to him that they were fleas on a gear, revolving quietly into the mechanism of earth and sky. There seemed little difference between the dusty, insect-smeared glare of the windshield and the yellow glow behind his eyelids. Inside was soon warmer, more comfortable. Nagging thoughts became murmurs here. Then with a sudden swerve left, free of the endless turn, he was awake and frightened. He was pointed at the opposite shoulder. Drawing them back across the center line, he groped for a cigarette. He must be deliberate. He had come too far.

The curve took him out from the sun's direct glare, exposing the vast stretch of road leading to the top of the next hill. The view wasn't encouraging: a barn listing atop the swaying corn, a house tiny on a ridge in the distance, and a grazing field with a few head of cattle. Not a soul in sight. A farm road appeared and ran parallel to the highway for a short bit and then veered off into the stalks to vanish. This was nowhere. To pull off would only delay his fatigue. He needed coffee. One face without rancor. There had to be something soon. A billboard, half-hidden by trees at the top of the next rise, mocked him: fifteen miles to pecan pie.

It wasn't the thought of food that made him patient, made him pace himself over this last stretch. It was the notion of the café. People would be eating and talking. There would be waitresses, and a cash register ringing. The air-conditioned interior would feel like cool water, a summer swim, a relief from his scorched loneliness. Perhaps he would even be hungry. His stomach was flat and meaningless, as it had been since they left. This wasn't like him. He had always been able to eat. Whatever the problem was, he'd have to worry about it later – right now it was a blessing. He couldn't afford cold toast. And

Martha wasn't about to treat him. He glanced at her curled up against the passenger door and wished he were already there.

The sign for the turn off had nearly rushed by before he saw it. He took the exit slowly, but felt Martha stir despite his caution. Don't wake up, damn it, he thought. The gas station he knew he should stop at was passed with only a fleeting hesitation. The arrow on the fuel gauge had touched the top of the empty mark a few miles back. He would wake her and get it filled before they left. The restaurant was just a few yards away anyway. As he neared the lot and the little building, he glanced back to the sign to verify that he had come to the right place. It was an old drive-in. The original colors of orange and brown were faded to pumpkin and mud and each spot where a logo might be expected was covered with a square white sign bearing the new name: Andy's. There were no other cars. A small open window and a teenage girl inside reassured him that it wasn't abandoned. He parked and Martha woke up.

"Why are you stopping?" she asked.

"Coffee."

"Here?"

He got out without answering.

After checking Lisa, who was asleep in the back seat, Martha climbed out as well and was soon at his heels as he approached the window. She was ordering coffee for both of them before he could open his mouth.

"You want something to eat too?" she asked.

He looked at her in surprise and shook his head.

Martha paid and they carried the Styrofoam cups to a picnic table out under the awning. Neither spoke. David punched grooves into the lip of his cup with his thumbnail.

"I'm not over being mad at you," she finally said.

"So what else is new?"

"I guess I've no right to expect better treatment than what I've gotten. I should've known something was wrong after what Toni told me. But me, I like to think the best of folks."

"What are you talking about?"

"Toni told me the whole sordid story about you and your father. How you got this." She took his hand and turned it over to expose the long scar across his palm. He pulled away from her. "Had I known you're one of those people that has no control over themselves, I wouldn't have agreed to let you drive me."

David was dumbfounded.

"I probably could have helped you, if you wanted it — " she continued.

"What do you want?" he asked.

"I want to get to Nashville in one piece."

"This is the first time today you've been civil to me. Just say what's on your mind."

"I want to know what Kathy told you. I can't have you driving, thinking all sorts of crazy things that she put in your head. There's no telling what you might decide to do."

"I'm not going to do anything! I'm going to finish this fucking trip and disappear."

"What did she tell you?"

"She said you killed George."

"And you believed her."

"Her more than you."

"I loved George!"

David clenched his teeth. He wanted to scream at her: She told me that too, you bitch! But he didn't say any more. He didn't want a confrontation. He wanted to be left alone.

"I know what she told you! She tried to sell the same cock and bull story to my brother! And you believe her!" Suddenly aware of how loud she had become, she lowered her voice to a hissing whisper and furtively glanced about.

There wasn't anyone in sight. "She tell you I was holding Lisa for ransom? That she has to sell herself to buy her daughter back?"

"No."

"She wanted you to help kidnap Lisa."

The look on his face must have given him away.

"So?" she asked.

"I thought about it."

"You just try it. I'll have the cops on you so fast it'll make your head spin."

"I'm not going to do anything."

"I'm not stupid," she said.

"What would I do with an upset three-year-old?" His flimsy bravado was quickly crumbling.

"You sleep with everything as it is," she said.

"What?"

Her eyes didn't quite look back.

"Who are you talking to?" he demanded.

"You. There isn't anybody else here, is there? I know this won't mean anything to you, but I'm the only stability she's got in the world. Children need that. They got to know what's up and what's down." She threw up her hands. "I don't know why I bother. You're already convinced I'm a liar."

"Maybe you both..." A blue pickup, like the one Kathy had been driving, rolled by on the empty street. He stared. The sunlight on the windshield made it impossible to see inside. He waited for the open side window and the arm that rested there to come abreast of them. The arm seemed flecked with something – hair or suntan lotion – he couldn't tell. The cab sailed into the forest of shadow beneath a large oak and then was past. All he had seen was a hat. It had to be a man.

"What's the matter?" she asked and turned. The truck was gone. "Looking for someone?"

"No."

"Who do you think you're fooling?" She was angry. "I'm the one that raised her. I've put up with almost twenty years of her lies and deceits. You don't think I know what's going on this very instant."

"You tell me. I don't know what the fuck is going on."

"Oh God, Davey. I wish we could start over somehow. Go back to when we left New Orleans – except this time we won't stop at the farm. I really thought you were something. Couldn't we pretend that?"

"No."

Her jaw hardened once again.

"I don't see how you can believe her. All those hysterics of hers – that's not grief. If you knew what it was like to lose someone you'd know the difference."

"What makes you think I don't?"

She reached for his hand. He hesitantly drew away.

"You're still young and mixed up. You don't know if you're coming or going..."

He stood up.

"I know you're the crazy one here!" he said.

Then he was walking away. He rounded the corner of the building. Her face was still before him, her voice still in his head. God damn her! He knew what grief was! Hadn't he crossed the creek and climbed the slope to Caroline's front porch! He couldn't have left without saying goodbye. He should have! He should have ducked and run and spent the rest of his life feeling guilty rather than know, rather than remember the look in her eyes. It wasn't his fault!

But it was, wasn't it? The deepening red of the dishrag wound around his hand was his shame made real. She had been too frightened to even ask what he had done. His hideousness was apparent. 'Don't look,' he had whispered. What stupidity! He shouldn't have come.

"Don't look at me." It was a game they knew. She would face away, and with his lips close to her ear, he would quietly describe what she could see if she had his eyes. When his voice couldn't find the sounds she touched his arm.

"What am I looking at?" she asked.

He had dripped blood on the grass.

"The yard stretches down to a barbed wire fence. The posts are rotted and crooked and there's a hayfield beyond that... Caroline, I'm going away for a while."

"You're hurt."

"Something's happened," he said.

"I... I thought we were getting married."

"I'll write you. If you still want me, I'll send for you."

"Have you..." She turned. "Stay. If I can't help you, who will?"

"You can't fix this."

"Give me your hand."

"No." He stood.

She lifted the open book from her lap.

"There's a word here I'm having trouble with."

"No."

"You never really wanted to help me," she said with a nervous smile. "You were always ready to go play with the boys."

"I'll write. I promise."

She might have said 'You're deserting me,' but the words couldn't surface in the silence. Her face wasn't willing to believe it yet.

He hadn't believed it either. They should have been married. What was he doing here? He had stopped at the back screen of the restaurant. A deep-fat fryer vat filled with oil sat on the ground before him. Inside, a boy in an apron and white cap was leaning back, cleaning his fingernails with a knife. David moved away from the rancid grease, afraid that he might be seen. The odor remained with him like a scar. When he was fifteen, dumping the fryers at the end of the week had been his job: he was the biggest. Carrying it chest high, the stench rose to his nostrils and eyes like heavy smoke. His face was left crusty and sour. He hadn't minded. It was home and work. And there was Caroline. He suddenly thought of that dumb kid he had worked with, the one who had something to prove and had tried to carry it out one night. He had come back drenched, with most of his arms and chest burned, and tears in his eyes because he had made a mess on the pavement. David wiped his own moist eyes, feeling stupid. He just couldn't get it right.

Dumping grease was all he was good for. He walked toward the oil drums sitting on the outer edge of the drive. A rat ran from beneath the dumpster as he approached, but he scarcely noticed it. The drum they used for the oil was easy to find: the lip was crusty with thickened drippings. Leave it alone, something told him, but he couldn't. He stared at the dark placid surface and was ready to reach into it, gather it up and spread it over his face and hair, ready to smear it on his skin and wallow in it. Make himself horrible, frightening. This was where he belonged, wasn't it? In the filth. Everything was undone. He was the monster, the burned, the stupid. He would take it all away from them.

If he could move. The slabs of meat hanging from his wrists were heavy with decay, ready to drop to the cement. He was rotting from the inside out. Muscle was dissolving. A sudden turn might send a piece flying. He held his breath and prayed for the blood to flow back into his withered skin. A sudden scurry of movement made him leap back, his heart seized, horrified that he might find a rat dragging away a blue hand. But it was just a rat. And then he knew what was killing him. They were burning the flesh of his thigh, poisoning him. He pulled the papers, Kathy's note and Caroline's letter, from his pocket and ripped them to shreds, throwing them into the grease. They didn't sink. He was frantic. He found an old broom and tried to push the pieces into the muck. Stirring didn't work either. He was soon laughing. It didn't matter! He was free, wasn't he? He let the broom handle drop to the rim of the drum. On the dark surface the remaining shards of paper had become translucent with the oil. The ink resembled the purple veins of an old woman's arm. He should have been exalted and dizzy. Couldn't we pretend that, he thought ruefully?

He turned. Martha had to be tired of waiting. He was ready he guessed — and he didn't want her coming back here to get him. As he crossed, there was the muffled roar of an engine being gunned out front, beyond the corner. The car and trailer suddenly swung into the back drive. Martha was at the wheel. He paused, expecting her to slow and stop for him. Tires squealed. He waved. The glaring windshield rushed him. She wasn't going to stop! He jumped away. The pavement came up hard and grinding and he rolled. The back corner of the trailer sideswiped the oil drum next to him as it was flung by. Rubber screeched again as the car made the second turn and was gone. He lay there dazed, his arms scraped and aching. Then he realized that the car had died. All he could hear was sputtering and the ignition grinding. He scrambled to his feet and tried running after her. His knee hurt.

The car had stopped at the edge of the lot near the road. She was trying to get it started again. When the engine did turn over it would merely quiver a few times and die. He slowed to catch his breath. She wasn't going anywhere. This was ludicrous. He knew he should be outraged. She had tried to kill him. But he just couldn't care. They were both such lousy jobs. As he reached for the door handle, she fumbled to lock it. He was quicker and yanked it open. Her hands were up in front of her face. Lisa was in the back seat trembling.

"The car got away from me. I was trying to stop. Honest!" she said.

"Give me some money."

"What?"

"You're out of gas."

"You're not angry?"

"You don't have to kill me," he said almost mournfully. "I'm already dead."

Her face turned white.

"The money," he said.

She reached for her purse and clawed through it until she found her wallet. When she handed the whole thing to him, he pulled out a few bills and gave it back. In a minute he would cross the road to the station and see if he could borrow a gas can, but for now it seemed they had come to a complete halt, as if the trip would end here in their fearful vows to one another. He waited for her to say something. It didn't matter what. He understood her too well.

Chapter Fourteen

The yellow sun was melting behind the base of the radio tower on the hill. The flashing red sparks on the girders above formed the first chattering constellation of the deepening sky. This was Nashville. Headlights and the neon placards of the street rising into night hurried to meet them. The bobbing flow of taillights drew him on as the other colors failed. And he would glance back one last time for the blue hood and cab of the pickup before it was lost for good. It would become what it had always been: his companion, a moth about a porch light, a mother scorched with grief and searching for her child. Kathy had followed them. She had never left them. And he knew suddenly that he should be gone before she arrived. So that he wasn't mistaken for something else in the dark.

In the next block the dark cutout of a greyhound bounded across a bright sign above the bus station. This was easy. He wouldn't have to ask Martha for directions. All he had to do was get to the opposite side of the street. Flipping the turn signal, he edged over into the left lane.

"Where are you going? It's straight up this way," she said.

"To the bus station."

"You can at least drive us to the trailer."

"You can. It's not far."

"In all this traffic? And who's going to help me unload?"

He was circling the block.

"Look," she said, digging in her purse. "Here's a fifty dollar bill. You can have it the minute we pull in at the trailer."

"The deal was Nashville and a bus ticket. It won't cost you as much."

"I'm not buying you a ticket!"

"We'll stop. You buy the ticket and I'll drive you the rest of the way," he said wearily.

"I'm not buying you a ticket! You can drive around till kingdom come."

"Put the fifty on the dash. I want it when we get there or I'll back out again. And I'm not unloading a god damn thing."

She did as he asked.

"Your pants are on fire or something?" she asked.

Without replying, he turned back up the hill until he reached the street he had just left. The sign, still visible in his side mirror, gradually dissolved into the blur of the other meaningless lights.

Was she still with them? If she had seen their detour, she would have to assume it had been intentional. Why shouldn't she believe he was on Martha's side? The pistol in her glove compartment seemed to loom larger and larger. And it occurred to him that it didn't belong to the uncle, left there for rattlesnakes – it was hers. And that she had brought it for a reason. He had been her stopgap, her excuse, her last hesitation. If he had helped her. Now there was nothing. He felt as if he should quickly paint a large sign to hang around his neck: I didn't help Martha either. He had yet to tell her they were being followed. Wasn't that enough?

Damn them! He still felt like the missing piece. All he would have to do is hang around until the truck appeared, grab Lisa and throw her to her mother. No violence. No murder. Kathy could get away guilt free. He would save Martha's life and probably his own. Some hero. Rescuing the baby from the ogre so he could hand her over to the man-eater. It wasn't much of a solution. He would be doing good just to get away whole.

"I hope you're happy," Martha said. "That fifty was meant to put food on the table. I don't know if we've got enough to feed us until I can find a job."

He refused to answer. Who was she kidding? Of all the little girl's problems, starving wasn't one of them. Anyway, it wasn't his responsibility to feed her!

He knew what he was going to do. He was going to run. If he ever got there. The car was sputtering and groaning. Even with the gas pedal all the way to the floor, they were still slowing. He pulled as close as he could to the curb, shifted into low, and continued at a crawl. Horns protested from the traffic whizzing by. By the time they reached their turn off, the sun was gone, leaving only a milkish glow below the clouds. Three blocks down the side street and there was the entrance to the trailer park. He took this last corner slowly, so that he could check behind for headlights. There were none. Where was she? What was she waiting for? He hit the first speed bump unaware and the trailer hitch scraped noisily.

"Watch what you're doing," Martha said.

"You want to do it? I'll get out right here!"

He bounced carefully over the next one and she pointed to the mobile home. It was a wide dark block sitting atop a small rise. The grass was only beginning to get high, as if it had been mowed sporadically while she was gone. Pulling into the drive, he wearily shifted into Park and took the bill from the dash. The engine continued to chug a little after he shut it off. Then everything was quiet. Climbing out of the car was going to be the hard part. What if she was already out there?

"You mind waiting long enough for me to have a look inside?" Martha asked.

"I've got to go."

"Oh great! What if there some bums camping out in there? I'm supposed to run them off all by myself?"

"A few winos shouldn't scare you."

"David. I'm making a reasonable request."

"Do it quick."

She got out with Lisa and stopped beside the car.

"Well, come on!"

Opening the door, he scooted out and slowly stood up. He had been holding his breath, waiting for a pop and the quick hiss of a bullet. His eyes were swimming with stars. He followed them to the front step, distractedly looking back at the entrance of the trailer park.

"She won't show," Martha said.

"What?"

"She's afraid of me. Whatever she said, she won't follow through."

Why did he believe her? Martha fumbled with the keys. In the dim light he could see her hands trembling as she unlocked the front door.

The air inside was stale and hot. Martha set about opening drapes and windows in the living room and then disappeared into the dark hole of the kitchen. He reached for the light switch even though he knew it wouldn't work. After a moment's clatter and the scrape of a match, she emerged with two brightly burning candles. The aura from the unwavering flames cast the room in deep shadow. Lisa's hand found his pants leg and held on. He looked down at her in surprise.

"It's spooky, isn't it?" he said.

He took her hand in his rather than try to drag her alongside as they followed Martha down the narrow hallway. They opened windows as they went. David waited

216

at the bedroom door while Martha checked the closets and bathroom. Then she turned and frowned.

"I have one more favor to ask you," she said. "Then you can go."

"And one more after that."

"Actually two, but that's all. I promise." She repressed a smile.

"Why should I?"

"Because you're a good person."

Because you can't help yourself, she might have said. He didn't want to ask what the favors were.

"Well?" he said.

"Just a box of linen from the trailer. And the gas hooked up – so I can cook and we can take baths. It might be days before the gas company can send someone."

"I'm leaving now. You can forget it."

"Aren't you supposed to stay until Kathy shows up?"

"I never agreed to help her."

"I could almost believe you," she said.

Releasing Lisa's hand, David turned and walked back toward the dark living room. He could hear Martha following, but he wouldn't look back.

"Why don't you spend the night? You must be tired. You could take the first bus in the morning. They wouldn't fire you for missing one day."

He bowed his head.

"It might be roman– it could be fun camping out by candlelight."

He paused by the door and finally looked at her. The weight of her deep eyes was painful. What willpower he might have had was strewn behind him on the street and the highway. It was so much easier when she was mad at him. He didn't have to see her.

"I need to go."

"You know," she spoke softly, timidly, "sometimes so many bad things can be healed by a simple kiss."

He couldn't answer. He couldn't.

"Never mind," she said.

"Do you know what box the linen is in?" he heard himself ask.

"Sure."

The street outside was empty and quiet as they went down to the trailer. Lisa was staying close by his side. Martha retrieved a flashlight from the car while he unlocked the doors and swung them open. The white beam hesitated over one colorless cardboard box in the corner and then on one further back in the jumble.

"I'm not sure which it is," she said.

He tried the one in the front first.

"I thought you were sure."

He unloaded and rearranged things until he could free the other box. Under the light, the sheets looked like spun sugar.

"Anything else you want?" he asked. There was a car approaching. He looked, but the sound went away again.

"That one. I think its bathroom things."

He handed it out to her and then picked up the smallest one he could find and gave it to Lisa. She marched ahead of them back to the front step.

They unloaded their boxes on the living room floor.

"Can you wait while I put her down?" Martha asked.

David nodded.

Martha quickly slid the sofa cushions on to the floor, covered them with a sheet and began undressing her.

"Barbie."

"What did you say, honey?" Martha asked her.

"Her doll," he replied, "I'll go get it."

"Wait. Grandma will bring it back when she comes. In you go."

She held up the second sheet for her and tucked it up around her chin.

"We'll be back in a little bit. We're not going far."

Martha ushered him outside.

"I don't want her to get used to sleeping with things in the bed," she told him.

"Surely one doll wouldn't hurt."

"You don't have to sleep with her. Oh, you'll need a wrench. Be right back."

She returned to the trailer, carefully closing the screen after her so that it wouldn't make any noise. David strolled over to retrieve the gas attachment. Fireflies blinked here and there above the grass. It was quiet. Only the hum of the busy street nearby and the glow hiding the stars told him where he was. And he knew what was to happen next. Looking for it from the outside, from Kathy and her gun, had just been an excuse, a delay. A way to avoid the truth. Martha was going to kill him now. That was why he was waiting, wasn't it? Why wasn't he frightened?

She came out and again closed the screen quietly. The monkey wrench was held out for him to take. She was a dark silhouette against the iridescent sky. The yellow light behind the screen flickered.

"Now what?" he asked.

"Now you scoot under the trailer and hook this up."

"Where's the gas turn-off?" he asked.

She led him around the corner to the front of the trailer and showed him the meter. The little metal lever was in the off position. He touched it. This was no insurance. He would have laughed at himself if he weren't so numb. Her eyes were hidden in shadow. Was she smiling? A box of kitchen matches was in her hand. She wasn't even trying to hide them from view. He was dreaming.

"You know I'm not staying," he said.

"Yes."

"Are you out to scare me?"

"What do you mean?"

"Kathy was right, wasn't she?"

"I know who you are now," Martha said.

"What?"

219

She didn't answer. David looked away distracted. It didn't matter, he reminded himself, nothing mattered. There could be stars though. The red sparks of the radio tower above them blinked off and then on and then off again. They were too far – just tiny flecks swimming in the haze – they couldn't touch him. He was light-headed and confused. What was the next thing to do?

"You'll have to hold the flashlight on me so I can see," he said.

As she went to car, he knelt down and peered into the wide hole where the trailer's skirting had been removed. It was black. Too dark for anything except spiders. Too dark for anything really alive. Martha had returned and turned the light on him. His shadow had already started in. He got down on his belly and dragging the attachment in one hand and the wrench in the other, he crawled and wiggled back to where the beam illuminated the gas line. Hooking the attachment to the bottom of the trailer was done easily enough considering the awkward space he had to work in and the clumsiness of the brace on his finger. He tightened the connecting bolt until he couldn't move it any longer. The flashlight wavered.

"Hold it still," he yelled.

The light went off.

He froze. There was a faint creak from the front of the trailer. Although he couldn't hear it, he could feel the rushing gas out the end of the unattached line. In a moment he could smell it. He panicked. Groping in the darkness, he found the loose line and tried to fit it to the opening on the attachment. He fumbled. He couldn't do it! There wasn't time! He was crying. Slamming the wrench against the metal, he hit his own hand. Pain shot up his arm. The finger in the brace throbbed. He rolled back, holding it to his chest. Martha's feet were outside in the grass.

"What are you waiting for?" he screamed. "Do it! Go ahead!"

He was getting sick from the gas. There was a scrape of the match. Then nothing. He held his breath. Nothing.

"Do it!" he shouted.

The match fell to her feet and went out. Another one was struck. He scrambled for the opening. Five feet. Three feet. He grabbed the edge of the skirting as the tiny flame flew by his face. He covered his head. There was a tremendous thump and the ground and the trailer and the skirting jolted. Then nothing. Then the sound of her feet on the front step. David was outside, rolling in the grass, trying to catch his breath. He was numb. He didn't know if he had been blown out or if he had crawled out. Nothing hurt except his finger. He was alive.

His heart was pounding. His head was swimming. But he had to get up. The gas line was still open. He could hear the hissing now. Groggily, he got to his knees, then his feet. Everything ached. His head the worst of all. Nothing was broken or bleeding. He stumbled to the front of the trailer, found the lever and pressed it back to its original position. The hiss stopped. Leaning with his hand on the wall, he tried to raise his head. The vise on his temples tightened and the darkness seemed to rush at him. He paused to let it pass. He was up. He had to stay up.

He started for the front door. Fury was all he had left. She was standing just inside the screen, waiting for him. She had been waiting forever. Her knife gleamed in the candlelight.

"Don't you come in here!" she yelled. The door handle didn't move when he pulled. "I'll kill you!"

He took it in both hands and yanked it from its lock. When the screen swung back in his way, he grabbed the top and twisted it outward. A hinge screeched free of the doorjamb. She was pushing the inner door against his arm. He kicked and she stumbled back. He was inside.

Martha lunged at him, the knife high. He caught her wrist in midair and turned the hand until she lost her grip. The knife hit the floor. There was a red streak across his forearm. He released her to cup the wound. She backpedaled. Turning the hand up revealed just a bit of blood on his palm. It wasn't deep.

"Get out of here! We don't want you here!" She was screaming hoarsely.

She hurled a lamp at him. It hit his arm and fell, shattering on the carpet. She threw books from a tabletop. Snatching up a vase, she attacked again.

"Get out!"

She whacked the arm he had raised. And then hit him again. He reached for the vase and tore it from her hands. She started in with her bare fists. She was flailing her arms and kicking when he tried to hold her wrists, so he seized her neck and shook her.

She was soon clawing at his hands. Her face was contorted, her eyes bulging. Her mouth was open to scream, but nothing came out. He knew the damage he was doing, saw the awful moment of her death. And he didn't want to quit. He wanted to wring her out, twist the neck until the head turned grey and breathless. Squeeze those disapproving eyes into oblivion. Her knees were faltering. Lisa was suddenly at his leg, hammering at him with her small fists.

"Stop it. Stop!" she cried.

He looked from her back to Martha. There was pleading in both their eyes. He was cheated, humbled. They weren't going to satisfy him. Finishing her would be messy and mean. What was he doing? Was he crazy too? He released her. And then shoved her as hard as he could. She fell to the floor.

"You've made me as nuts as you!" he screamed.

She put a hand to her throat and tried to say something, but couldn't get the sound out. Her arms were reaching for Lisa. The little girl ran to her. Once she was folded in against her chest, against the bruised neck, Martha edged away and picked up the vase that had fallen to the floor. The jagged glass of its end sparkled in the candlelight.

"You're not my mother!" he shouted.

"You..." Martha croaked. "You go away."

"I'm not George!"

"Evil. The devil come to punish."

"No!"

"Go away." Her voice was an exorcism. Had she a cross to hold against him, he would have burst burning from the trailer. She was everything he had destroyed now resurrected. He couldn't have killed her. She would have sat up bloated and bruised and pointed her finger just as she was doing.

"No! You don't know who I am!"

If he remained, he would break things, tear the trailer down around them, and send all of them up in flames. He found the doorway and was stumbling down the stairs.

The last step thudded behind him. He glanced back to find the source of the odd sound, but found nothing. The doorway was empty. He had to get out of here. Martha might decide to come after him. When he turned to run he saw the pickup. It was sitting at the bottom of the drive. At first, that was all he could see. That was enough. He froze. Where was she? There was another thud on the ground beside him, then the pop of the revolver. The line in the grass and the noise led him to Kathy. She was standing in front of the car. The pistol was raised. Pointed at his head.

"Don't shoot me, goddamn it!"

She remained motionless, mute.

"I'm not George! I'm David Jacks! You hear me?"

The world was frozen with him in place. The gun wasn't lowered. The gun didn't go off. He wasn't breathing. And then he exhaled, slowly, silently. He wanted to live.

"I haven't done anything to you. I'm going to walk away. Martha and Lisa are inside."

Still no answer.

"I'm walking now."

He moved his feet carefully, stepping sideways. With each movement of his legs he saw and felt the trigger tighten, the strain of her finger squeezing it back. He was halfway across the yard. The barrel had followed him. There was a noise from inside the trailer. Please not now! Stay put a few more seconds! He had reached the street. The pick-up was barring his escape.

"I'm not touching the truck," he yelled. "I'm going around."

Had she lowered the revolver? He couldn't tell in the darkness. Could he run? He had to run. He was going to die. He broke, running as hard as he could. Not fast enough. Faster. His feet would bury the sound of the shot. He would die not knowing. Each pounding foot took him further from harm. He reached the park entrance, well out of sight of the trailer, and grabbed the gate pole as if it were a mast he would hold to ride out a storm. Two shots echoed over the arc of dull sky. The trailer.

"God!" he cried.

The third shot rang like the solitary chime of a clock tower in the first hour of early morning. Only silence came after.

Chapter Fifteen

The high vaulted terminal seemed a sea of white light. Against the rows of blue plastic seats, the vending machines and the worn tiles, David was small and growing smaller. People were coming and going from the gates, some were waiting with suitcases or backpacks positioned close; others, with faces like dirty erasers, were there for the night, their heads already nodding crookedly into their chests. Moving across the wide floor brought glances from the open eyes, then startled looks, and then averted faces when he gazed back in defiance. What were they looking at? He glanced down at his clothes. His shirt was dirty and streaked with grass stains, his pants ripped and oil stained. He was filthy. His face was probably the same or worse. He had become the monster he had wished to be. Let them stare. Let them see the damage he could do. Fuck them. He approached the ticket counter. The little fat woman behind the counter finally noticed him, and after examining him, moved further away to shuffle papers on a desk top. He cleared his throat. She pretended not to notice him.

"Excuse me," he said loudly.

"Yes?" she said without moving closer.

"I'd like to buy a ticket for New Orleans."

"Do you have any money?"

He had become one of the bums here. He had no rights, he was impressing no one. He was invisible.

"Yes."

She hesitantly returned to the counter and consulted a schedule book.

"Well, there's one leaving in twenty minutes at Gate 13."

He laid the fifty-dollar bill before him.

"I don't always look like this," he said. "There was a gas explosion. I need to be back at work tomorrow morning."

She slid the ticket and his change toward him.

"Is there a rest room where I can get cleaned up?"

"Over there. If you're hurt, you should go to the hospital."

"I'm all right, I think. I was under this trailer trying to hook up a gas line. A woman threw a match at me."

The look on her face told him he should shut up.

"I'm not a mess normally. Sorry if I bugged you."

"Sure. The rest room's over there."

"Thanks," he said and left to find the men's room. Entering, he turned the corner and came face-to-face with what everyone had been staring at. His cheeks and forehead were smeared with dirt. Closer examination revealed streaks of something resembling dried blood. His hair was matted and greasy. There was a slash on his neck. He pulled a handful of paper towels from the dispenser, wetted them in a sink and began to wash up. The skin beneath the grime was gray and sagging with fatigue. His eyes were swollen. It was hard to recognize any of himself in the reflection. The soft chin and lips were lost in a new grimace he didn't know. He was getting jowls. They would be like his father's – he was inheriting his face! It wasn't pretty. And it was too old to be his. The harsh fluorescent light wasn't the only thing that made him pallid. He looked

226

as though he had just seen the creature he had wished he could be. What had they done to him?

"Stupid question," he murmured to the man in the mirror. Still, he wasn't prepared for this. He stuck his head under the open tap and let the cold water rush about his ears. His head was throbbing when he straightened up. A few more paper towels from the dispenser dried his hair, and he dug for his comb. Caroline's letter was gone. He patted his empty pockets and then remembered that he had destroyed it. What was he thinking of? He ran the comb through his hair. George wouldn't have been concerned with a dumb letter. It wouldn't have mattered. So what if it had taken her hours: forming the 'R's and the 'S's so they went in the right direction. He sighed. Who was he kidding? He could close his eyes right now and see her freckled hand wrapped around a pencil. Who said he wanted to be George anyway?

He wasn't sure who he wanted to be.

Perhaps it didn't matter. Up there on the hill, when the sound of the crickets and distant traffic returned, and he had caught his breath, he thought of going back. Anyone would have. To make sure the little girl was all right. To prevent a murder if it hadn't already happened. To serve as witness. But he hadn't. He did what he had always done well. He turned and walked away. There was no excuse except his own fear. He was certain he would find all three of them dead. He could even see his own body stretched out beside them. If Kathy or Martha were still alive, it would have come true. That was enough of a nightmare. He wanted to wake up now. He could figure out the rest later.

If he could. He knew what he didn't want: everything that had happened since the day he had left home. Even poor little Lisa. He couldn't have saved her. She wasn't his to save. Damn them! All he had tried to do was fix things. Sure. All you wanted was family. It didn't matter what shape. Hope you're satisfied.

He shook his head. There had been a time when you could fix things, but not anymore.

So now he was dead. He pulled out a few more towels and wetted them to wipe off his clothing. It didn't help much, the spots remained, the dirt smeared and now he had dark splotches left by the water. At least those would dry. He cleaned the cut on his forearm. A bit of fresh blood seeped up, but a moment of pressure with the towel stopped it. Still can bleed, he told himself. He took one last look in the mirror, found the same ugliness he had found earlier and turned to go. Maybe he wasn't dead, just maimed. And a damn fool.

A fool capable of anything, he reassured himself. He returned to the ticket counter. The little fat woman sighed.

"I want to trade this ticket for another one."

"It's a perfectly good ticket."

"For a different place. I want to go to Nannerton, Indiana. It's a little town outside of Evansville."

She checked her schedule books.

"The bus is boarding at Gate number two in twenty minutes. Are you sure this time? We can't keep exchanging tickets for you."

"I'm not sure, but give me the ticket anyway."

"If you're going to be a problem, I'll have to call the security guard."

"This will be the last time you see me. I promise."

She handed over the new ticket and the difference in cash.

"You've been wonderful," he said and went to sit in front of the gate. It was a long wait. This was scarier than he could have ever imagined.

When they began boarding, he nervously got in line before the bus, and took his turn climbing up the two large steps into the dark interior. The seat in front across from the driver was empty, so he stretched out there and watched the driver outside take the last of the passenger tickets, help load the last of the bags and close the luggage compartments and finally climb up into the bus himself. The engine roared. The front door was closed and the bus backed out of the stall. When the bus turned onto the street, David spotted the patrol car parked in front of the entrance. The two cops were getting out, slipping their billy clubs into their belts and heading inside. He slouched down in his seat. He had no idea if they were there for him or not. Martha or Kathy could have called them to blame the whole thing on him. A neighbor might have seen him running away. He did know that the woman at the ticket counter would remember the bus he had boarded. If the bus were stopped, he would just have to explain his side of it and hope for the best. It was probably too late for him to go home anyway. He crossed his fingers and held them hard in his lap until the last lights of the city dropped away and the bus was tunneling deeply into the country night.

The End

A Screened Porch in the Country

All of them are sitting
Inside a lamp of coarse wire
And being in all directions
Shed upon darkness
Their bodies softening to shadow, until
They come to rest out in the yard
In a kind of blurred golden country
In which they more deeply lie
Than if they were being created
Of Heavenly light.

Where they are floating beyond
Themselves, in peace,
Where they have laid down
Their souls and not known it,
The smallest creatures,
As every night they do,
Come to the edge of them
And sing, if they can,
Or, if they can't, simply shine
Their eyes back, sitting on haunches,

Pulsating and thinking of music.
Occasionally, something weightless
Touches the screen
With its body, dies,
Or is unmurmuringly hurt,
But mainly nothing happens
Except that a family continues
To be laid down
In the midst of its nightly creatures,
Not one of which openly comes

Into the golden shadow
Where the people are lying,
Emitted by their own house
So humanly that they become
More than human, and enter the place
Of small, blindly singing things,
Seeming to rejoice
Perpetually, without effort,
Without knowing why

James Dickey

If you enjoyed this book, please let others know by leaving a quick review on Amazon. Also, if you spot anything untoward in the paperback, get in touch. We strive for the best quality and appreciate reader feedback.

editor@thebookfolks.com

www.thebookfolks.com

Also by Dan McNay:

UNDER THE COLD STONES

Made in the USA
San Bernardino, CA
22 January 2018